What the critics are saying...

5 Hearts! "Cheyenne McCray has done it again! ...I highly recommend this book for the adventuresome reader and can't wait to see what Cheyenne McCray pens next." ~ *Angel Brewer, The Romance Studio*

5 stars! "Flaming! ... Readers of erotica will find Blackstar: Future Knight to be at the top of genre as an example of how erotic romance should be done." ~ *Johnna Flores, Coffee Time Romance*

4 Stars! "Blackstar: Future Knight is a roller coaster of ride. ...Blackstar is a definite keeper, with strong, engaging characters and sizzling passion." ~ *Niniri Theriault, The Road to Romance*

5 Roses! "Blackstar: Future Knight is full of all the things readers have come to expect from Cheyenne McCray: spicy hot love scenes, strong dynamic characters, and a solid plot. Fans and newcomers alike will not be disappointed with Ms. McCray's latest release." ~ *Cynthia, A Romance Review*

4 Hearts "Ms. McCray delivers a highly charged, well-crafted story that combines the elements of futuristic and romantic genres and delivers a great read for a cool fall day... This reviewer was captivated by the way Ms. McCray crafted her storyline and delivered a highly interesting, sexually charged ride that leaves the reader breathless, with a climactic ending that delivers a big bang." ~ *Dawn, Love Romances*

BLACKSTAR: FUTURE KNIGHT

Cheyenne McCray

Future Knight
An Ellora's Cave Publication, August 2004

Ellora's Cave Publishing, Inc.
1337 Commerce Drive
Stow, Ohio 44224

ISBN # 1419951084

Edited by: *Heather Osborn*
Cover art by: *Syneca*

Warning:

The following material contains graphic sexual content meant for mature readers. *Future Knight* has been rated *E-rotic* by a minimum of three independent reviewers.

Ellora's Cave Publishing offers three levels of Romantica™ reading entertainment: S (S-ensuous), E (E-rotic), and X (X-treme).

S-*ensuous* love scenes are explicit and leave nothing to the imagination.

E-*rotic* love scenes are explicit, leave nothing to the imagination, and are high in volume per the overall word count. In addition, some E-rated titles might contain fantasy material that some readers find objectionable, such as bondage, submission, same sex encounters, forced seductions, etc. E-rated titles are the most graphic titles we carry; it is common, for instance, for an author to use words such as "fucking", "cock", "pussy", etc., within their work of literature.

X-*treme* titles differ from E-rated titles only in plot premise and storyline execution. Unlike E-rated titles, stories designated with the letter X tend to contain controversial subject matter not for the faint of heart.

BLACKSTAR: FUTURE KNIGHT

Cheyenne McCray

Prologue

It really was their luck, to flee the destruction of Earth and find a haven such as Blackstar—itself on the very eve of destruction as well.

Adan Valnez paced the length of the well-guarded and secret travel chamber, ignoring his two companions. The walls were fine-hewn and crafted by expert woodworkers and gemlayers, talents nearly lost to Old Earth, but slowly making a comeback here on Blackstar. On Blackstar, things were more basic.

And even more dangerous.

Growling, Adan gripped the hilt of his sheathed sword while his companions waited for him to speak. His long dark hair swung well past his broad shoulders nearly to the small of his back, and his black eyes sparked with dark fire as he bit back the urge to smash his fist into something—anything. His breeches and tunic felt constricting, and his boots slammed against the wood floor like hammers on stone.

No words could express the dire dilemma now faced by the three Clans. And Adan was weary of dilemmas. He was more than ready to find a pleasure-partner, relieve the pressure in his loins, and drink fire ale until his mind sang. Gods knew his companions didn't hesitate to enjoy the amenities of their refuge. But he was Clan Leader, knight of the Blackstar Realm, and responsible for the welfare of all. Moreover, he took his responsibilities more seriously than Dominik and Dane, the other two Leaders and knights of the first order.

At the end of the chamber, a floor-length panoramic window revealed the winter-held valley, hugged by the Mirror Mountains. The range was so named because the mountains' crystals reflected the valley from the countless ice-laden snow trees, to the frozen lake, to the village. As Adan stopped his pacing, the crystals in the travel chamber seemed to blink in time with those on the slopes. The only warmth in this world was that within the Clans' buildings and homes, and the hot springs beneath the frozen lake.

Below the travel chamber, the Tower of Light glittered, and the village's white walls sparkled in the always gray light. Unconcerned with the ever-present threat of danger, most of the valley's residents went about their business, working in the mines, learning and practicing crafts and arts, tending crops in the greenhouses, patronizing the many establishments, and teaching children at their daily lessons.

Earth's remaining survivors, now a small community of less than five thousand, were fairly new residents of the refuge, at only one decade's time. The newcomers had christened the planet Blackstar because it had a natural shield that reflected the endless depths of space and grasped enough warmth from the planet's distant sun to keep the ice-world at a temperature where it still sustained life.

Luck. Yes. We were *lucky to find this place, all temper aside.*

Adan bit back a sigh.

No matter how advanced Old Earth's technology had become, Earth scientists had never discovered the wormhole that crouched in space waiting for its next meal. When Adan's people fled Earth during the Age of Sorcery and the end of most life on Earth, their spacecraft had been swallowed whole by the anomaly. By sheer fortune, when they were spit back out, the small planet had been discovered, and Blackstar was now home.

An occasional guardcraft zipped by the chamber's window as Adan resumed his pacing, and he heard one of his companions clear his throat. His knights patrolled the realm's borders, and guardcraft protected the citizens of Crystal Valley from ruthless beings that haunted the realm's minimal borders. Beings that did not want to share their world with outsiders—ice-ghosts who wished to conquer Adan's people.

From outside Adan heard the drone of the craft, and from inside the room, the constant hum of the time-arch. Adan finally glanced at the two other Clan Leaders, his partners and friends, who had come to aid him in the search for the hidden powercrystal.

Blond-haired, gray-eyed Dane had his feet up on the wooden meeting table, his arms crossed, his chair tipped back, and his gaze focused on Adan. Dominik—of equal stature as his companions, but dark-haired and green-eyed—rested one hip on the table and merely cocked an eyebrow at Adan's unusual restlessness. Each of them wore the uniform of the Blackstar Knight with the star and sword insignia on one sleeve.

"The draw of the crystal comes from Old San Francisco Providence, obliterated early in the Age of Sorcery." Adan raked his fingers through his dark hair. "The Cwen informed me that it was hidden in Earth's year

2010, long before the dividing of the continent. But finding the crystal will be like searching for a thimble in a hayfield."

"Needle in a haystack," Dominik corrected with a grin, but then his features grew serious. "What has the Sanor queen told you to make you so restless?"

Adan sighed. "Not much more than her usual pleas."

Dominik and Dane grunted in unison.

The Clan Leaders already knew much of what they needed to know. Two decades ago the powercrystal was spirited away for safekeeping on Earth of the past. The nearly destroyed peoples of Sanor had hidden the crystal to keep it from falling into the hands of a vicious Ice-Witch. It was said that the one crystal was stashed with another priceless Sanor treasure.

Adan had no interest in treasure. He only had interest in retrieving the crystal before the Ice-Witch Echna did. According to T'ni Lael, the Cwen—a refugee from the Sanor realm—the crystal held a great power that the Ice-Witch would use against Adan's people if she possessed it. The bitch would then be in a position to mount a full, and likely final, attack on Adan's people.

Aye, what fortune, to flee the destruction of Earth to fight yet another potentially cataclysmic battle. Maybe here, though, the Clans could truly make a difference. Maybe they could act fast enough and decisively enough to save Blackstar from the fate of Old Earth.

Adan braced his hands on the table and looked from Dominik to Dane. "The Cwen believes the Ice-Witch has learned the crystal's location and *when* the crystal was hidden. She will send warriors of her own to retrieve it. We must find the crystal first."

Dominik shook his head, his sharply angled face reflecting the severity of his emotion. "Damn."

With a slow nod, an unusually somber Dane agreed. "We waste time talking when you should be hunting."

The time-arch seemed to hum louder, as if emphasizing the urgency.

"Agreed." Adan pivoted from the table and strode to the arch at the end of the room. The time-arch was a carefully crafted doorway with glowing runes around the rounded opening. The closer Adan and his sword came to the arch, the brighter the runes shone.

Each man had been trained to use the arch countless times by T'ni Lael so that they had mastered the abilities required to reach into Earth's past. The time-arch was powered by timecrystals and thoughtpower. It took all three to power it, with Dane and Dominik manning the control panels while Adan traveled.

Adan bore a sword infused with the same powers as the time-arch, a sword that would guide him through time and to the draw of the crystal. But as T'ni Lael had cautioned, it would only lead him to the correct year, and close to the location. He would have to use his soul—and his heart—beyond that.

He nearly rolled his eyes at the thought of the Cwen's insistence that he would need to use his heart. His heart was long dead, his soul long closed off. His keen hunting abilities, his intelligence, and his natural leadership abilities would have to do.

Dominik and Dane each placed their palms on the twin control panels as Adan stepped through the golden shimmer. Adan nodded to each man and drew his sword, its own runes glowing in time with the time-arch's.

Adan concentrated on the draw of the *L'sen* Crystal, and then melded back in time.

Chapter One

I'm so pathetic. I have no life.

With a frustrated groan, Kara Marks leaned back on the couch and stared at the white whorls on her living room ceiling. She twirled her finger through one of her honey-blonde curls and popped her gum as her gaze returned to the papers scattered across her coffee table.

She glanced at a photo of her softball team from when she was an All-Star pitcher in high school. Next to it was a picture of her with several children from the local orphanage. When she could, she enjoyed spending time with the children, especially the youngest ones. Maybe she did have some life. She smiled.

Her eyes rested on the crystal cube-shaped paperweight next to the pictures. Inside the cube hung a silver-bordered pendant. Its silver chain glittered in the room's soft lighting. It was the only thing she had left from parents who had abandoned her shortly after her birth, but why they had made it into a paperweight, she'd never know.

And why she kept it was even more of a mystery.

Maybe it was because she found it amusing in some respects. The pendant almost looked like a penis, only much, much smaller.

While she studied the cube, she wondered when her life had become so freaking boring. Here she was on a Friday night, reviewing loan documents for clients instead of out on the town with some gorgeous guy. Well, at least a fairly decent-looking one. Right now just about any guy would do. Even doing one of her craft projects, like the art collages that plastered most of the walls in her home, would be better than nothing.

She turned her gaze to her living room's bay window and stared out at the gathering dusk. A streetlight stuttered and came to life, casting its yellow light over cracked sidewalks and patched pavement.

Other than spending some time at the orphanage, working out at the health club, and her job as a loan agent, she truly had no life. At least not an exciting one.

Her friends Jan and Sheri—well, they meant everything to Kara. The girls had lived in the same foster home until they were each shuffled off to separate families, but fortunately they'd all been raised in the San Francisco Bay Area and they'd been able to remain in close contact. The trio shared a bond that transcended the fact that they had all either been abandoned as toddlers, or had parents who'd passed away in tragic accidents.

Kara released her curl. It snapped back over her forehead, and in a restless movement she jumped to her feet. She felt antsy, like she could just about crawl out of her skin with boredom. The health club would definitely be a good choice right now to work off some of her restlessness. Maybe she'd strike up a conversation with one of the gorgeous guys who regularly worked out there. Or maybe not. All brawn, no brains...

But damn she needed to get laid. Just the thought of a good fuck made her nipples ache and her pussy throb. She loved sex—everything about it. The scent of a man's semen and of her own juices, the feel of a muscled chest beneath her palms, the feel of his hands upon her body. And being fucked...God, how she loved fucking.

She moved to the bay window and eased onto its royal blue padded seat, her legs tucked under her. It was her favorite place to sit and daydream. After pushing aside the sheer curtain, she placed her cheek to the glass so that she could see past her own reflection and into the night. Resting her head against the cool surface, she watched dry leaves swirl across asphalt in a gust of wind. A car passed by, its headlights piercing the dusk and the drone of its engine filling the night, and then the street was empty and quiet again.

Out of habit she twirled her finger in the curl that always hung over her forehead and popped her gum again. Maybe she'd call her friends and see if they'd like to go out to dinner, perhaps see a movie, or head to one of the nightclubs they enjoyed frequenting. When she wasn't working, Kara enjoyed flirting and teasing the opposite sex. As much as she enjoyed sex, she wasn't an easy lay, even though she'd had a few one-night stands. Rather, she was choosy—probably too choosy. She just couldn't find the right man, the man who really did it for her.

Maybe she just needed to dig out BOB, her battery operated boyfriend, and give herself a good orgasm. What would the neighbors think if she sat on her window seat and fucked herself with her vibrator while playing with her nipples? She had to grin at the thought of her neighbors directly across the street. Mrs. Hannigan would be bound to have a stroke, and Mr. Hannigan would probably enjoy the show.

A rumble rose in her belly and she realized she hadn't eaten for hours. She had spent the evening catching up on work she'd brought home. She was the top producing loan agent at the biggest bank in San Francisco, and she hated to lose one iota of the momentum that had taken her to that position. Yeah, she was definitely a workaholic, but she liked it that way. Working kept her from thinking about things that never were and things that never could be.

But sometimes she really wished she had chosen a more rewarding career, something that made a *difference* in someone's life. That she was truly making an important contribution.

Kara groaned. There she went again.

Just as she started to slip off the window seat to head into the adjacent kitchen, a shimmer above the sidewalk caught her eye—a golden gleam in the evening sky. Slowly she released her curl and stopped chewing her gum. The gleam was maybe ten feet from her living room window, and it was growing larger and larger.

And strangely, her pussy started to pulse and throb, a sensation that grew more intense the brighter the glow became. Ripples flowed through her body and she swore she was close to orgasm.

The golden light vanished and the ache in her pussy lessened.

A man's form appeared where the shimmer had been.

Kara squeezed her eyes shut then opened them again. He was still there.

Not real. This can't be real.

The guy, *who couldn't possibly be real*, held a sword with both hands on its hilt. He posed as if prepared to strike anyone who might be lurking behind bushes to either side of her window, looking like some kind of futuristic knight.

Heart pounding, Kara placed her hand flat against the windowpane, unable to tear her gaze from him. Black clothing molded athletic thighs, tapered hips, a large chest, and broad shoulders, and some kind of insignia was on the sleeve of his shirt, like he was a Green Beret or something.

Her eyes traveled to his face and her tongue darted out along her lower lip. The ache between her thighs magnified. Even though he wasn't what she considered classically handsome, he was delicious…long black hair way below his shoulders, a strong jaw, high cheekbones, a hawk-like nose, a hard masculine cut to his mouth, and intense penetrating eyes—

Eyes that were now focused directly on her.

Kara's hand moved to her throat. *Shit.* She slid off the window seat, stumbled, and almost fell. She backed away until she could no longer see the man, her heart pounding even faster than before.

What were you thinking, Marks? Some guy appears out of nowhere holding a sword, and you're sitting there thinking how hot he is?

She tried to remember if she'd locked the doors. As usual she hadn't set the alarm.

Kara whirled to run to the alarm control box and smacked into something solid.

She was trapped by strong arms and staring at a black-clothed chest. Too shocked to scream, Kara's eyes shot up to meet the gaze of the man from the street. He was even taller than she realized, several inches over her five feet eight, and he was better looking in person, in a ruthless sort of way. His scent of winter breezes and testosterone washed over her, and his black eyes were narrowed and focused on her face.

She gulped and swallowed her gum.

Terror combined with fury as she regained her senses. "Back off, creep!" At the same time she rammed her knee up toward his balls, she drew her arm back, clenched her fist, and aimed it toward his jaw.

In an easy movement he blocked her knee with his, caught both her wrists, and forced them behind her back. He bound her wrists in one of his big hands, drawing her tight against him, and he used his other to catch her chin.

Oh, shit.

"Listen, you sonofabitch," Kara said, struggling to free herself from the intruder's grasp and attempting to keep fear out of her voice. "You'd better get out of my house, *now.*"

Saying nothing, he simply studied her, turning her chin so that he could examine one side of her face, then doing the same with the other side.

Kara couldn't stop the trembling that took over her body. "Who are you?"

"I am Adan." His voice was deep and throbbing, and he had a strong accent that sounded European, yet different. Despite herself, Kara felt a flush from her belly to her pussy. "What is your name?" he asked.

She scowled. "Like hell I'm going to tell you."

The man called Adan's fierce expression remained as he moved his hand from her chin and reached for the single curl over her forehead. He tugged at it, watching closely as it sprang back into place when he released it.

What was he doing?

The female was beautiful and Adan regretted that he had no time to spend with an Earth woman of the past. Such was forbidden in most cases, and ill-advised in most others. Meddling in the timeflow beyond retrieval of items that shouldn't be here in the first place — now, that would be risky indeed.

And yet, from the fire lighting her green eyes to the angry set of her mouth to the softness of her fair skin... She smelled of peaches and springtime, felt small and soft within his arms, and he could easily imagine how much pleasure he could give her.

He couldn't help the feral smile that curved the corner of his mouth or the throbbing of his cock. *To tame this one would be both interesting and pleasurable.*

At the sight of his smile the female stilled. For the first time he saw genuine fear in her green eyes. "Are you going to hurt me?"

Frowning, Adan shook his head.

Her throat worked as she swallowed. "You're not going to rape me, are you?"

His frown turned into a fierce scowl. "I would never."

The woman took a deep breath and relaxed in his arms. "Then just let me go. Take whatever you want, I don't care."

Anger stirred in his gut and he growled at the insult. "I am no thief."

"Then what the hell do you want?" True confusion passed across her features and her voice climbed an octave. "Why are you in my home?"

With a sigh, Adan placed his fingers over her face and she flinched. "I am ensuring you will not remember what you saw...or me."

Her eyes widened, but as he used his thoughtpower, her eyelids drifted shut and she went limp in his embrace. For a moment he just held her, enjoying the feel of her soft body in his arms. He lowered his head and drew in the scent of her hair and felt his cock grow harder against her belly.

With another growl, he scooped her up in his arms, taking care not to bump into the squat table in front of the couch and upsetting the glass forms upon its surface. He laid the woman gently on the couch's cushions and she gave a deep, shuddering sigh.

Adan sank to one knee and studied the woman who so greatly intrigued him. Her hair hung in honey-blonde curls about her face; she had a delicate nose, and now had a slight pout to her full lips as she slept. He brushed his knuckles over her cheek, enjoying the feel of her skin against his. She gave a little sigh and a soft smile touched her mouth.

"What is your name?" he said, allowing his thoughtpower to draw the response from her.

"Kara," she murmured. "Kara Marks."

"A beautiful name," he said as he stroked her cheek again, "Kara Marks."

Her chest rose and fell with her deep even breathing, drawing his attention to the full breasts beneath her blouse. Unable to help himself, he trailed his fingers down the curve of her neck to her shoulder and paused. He longed to cup one breast and tease the nipple with his thumb, drawing it to a tight peak. Then he would suckle it through her shirt and she would moan and beg him for more. He would slip her jeans from her body and lap at the nectar between her thighs.

Aye, he could give her pleasure even as she slept.

But he would not. This woman would give herself to him willingly, or not at all.

Adan frowned at the turn of his thoughts. He wasn't here to have sex with any woman, and he would certainly never see this one again. He had to locate the crystal before the Ice-Witch Echna's warriors found it, and he had to do it soon.

Damn the ice-ghost bitches. The Ice-Witch's warriors were nearly as feral as their mistress.

He rose to a standing position and closed his eyes, trying to focus on the magic of his sword. His weapon hummed and the runes upon the blade glittered, but it told him no more than the fact that he was near the crystal. It could be feet away or a mile for all he knew.

Can it be in this woman's home?

Slowly he worked his way through the house, careful not to disturb any of Kara's possessions. The sword continued its light humming sound, but never gave him any indication that he had neared the crystal.

After he searched the home from basement to attic with no luck, he stopped at Kara's side and studied the sleeping woman. Desire rose up in him hard and fierce and he had the urge to scoop her up in his arms and spirit her away to Blackstar and to his bed. On his planet she would be a fair flower in a world of ice and snow. Would she wilt, or would she thrive?

What the devil are you thinking about Valnez?

With a growl he turned on his heel and strode toward the front door. He had to get his mind off his cock, back on his duty, and find that damn crystal.

* * * * *

Kara toyed with her linguini as she listened to Sheri's and Jan's chatter. It was early Saturday evening and they were at their favorite Italian restaurant. The serious one of the trio, Sheri had long, strawberry-red hair, as straight as Kara's was curly, and her eyes were a clear shade of gray. Jan on the other hand had freckles, wheat-brown hair, and blue eyes, and was the mischievous member of the group.

While her friends talked about their current boy toys and work, Kara's thoughts turned back to this morning. She'd woken on her sofa with her jeans and shirt on instead of her nightgown, and had no memory of how she'd gotten there. The last thing she remembered was sitting on her window seat, staring out into the darkness, thinking about getting off with her vibrator. Apparently she'd fallen asleep there and then dragged herself to the couch, she just didn't remember it.

But her dreams last night—the erotic visions kept replaying in her mind, over and over and her panties grew damp just thinking about them. In her dreams, a tall, dark, and rugged man had held her, stroked her, set her body on fire for him. She squirmed in her seat, her short, silky skirt riding up her thighs as she remembered the throbbing sound of his voice, the light brush of his knuckles...Adan. Her dream man had been *Adan*.

"*Kara.*" Sheri's voice jerked Kara's attention from her daydreams to her friends who were staring at her.

Kara dropped her fork to her plate. It clattered and bounced onto the red tablecloth, splattering a bit of white sauce from her linguini. Jan's mouth curved into a gamin grin, and Sheri raised her eyebrows.

"So who's Adan?" Jan asked, and Kara realized she must have said his name out loud.

She shrugged and tugged down on the hem of her short skirt. "No one."

Jan and Sheri exchanged glances before Sheri said, "No secrets, honey. You know the rules."

With a resigned sigh, Kara smiled. Yeah, she knew the rules. They'd been best friends for over twenty years, since they were toddlers, and had been through everything and anything together. "All right. This is going to sound silly, but it's just some guy I dreamed about last night."

Jan snickered and Sheri gave a motion of her hand telling Kara to go on. "This is a guy you met?"

"I wish." Kara picked up her fork and fidgeted with it. "He was totally hot."

"If a dream man is doing it for you, you really need to get out more." Jan gave a toss of her wheat-brown hair and signaled the waiter. "I think you need a drink and then a night out on the town. And probably a good fuck."

Sheri gave a solemn nod. "Definitely."

Kara had to laugh. "No doubt."

The girls giggled and chatted some more. Kara mentioned how much fun she'd been having with the kids at the orphanage, and Sheri and Jan were enthusiastic about going with her the next time.

After the waiter returned and had poured each of them a glass of wine, they raised their glasses to their favorite childhood toast. "All for one—except if we get caught in the boys' bathroom and then it's each girl for herself."

Just a few short hours later, Kara found herself tipsy and on her front doorstep with Paul, a guy she'd dated a few times and had run into at the nightclub. Paul was her height and sandy-haired, and he had an entirely sexy, lean and muscled body. Since she'd ridden with Jan and Sheri to the club, she had let Paul drive her home. But even as she dug her keys out of her purse and unlocked her door, she knew she didn't want to let him in.

The lock clicked and Kara let the keys dangle from it as she hugged her leather jacket closer around her and turned back to Paul. His blond hair gleamed gold in the streetlight and early fall wind teased the fine strands. He was definitely a good-looking man, but tonight he just wasn't doing anything for her. All night she had wished she would run into someone who looked like her dream man — tall with long dark hair and a hard edge, but sensual, too.

"Thanks for bringing me home." She leaned forward and gave Paul a light kiss. "Good night."

"Hey." Paul caught her arm and drew her closer to him. "Aren't you going to invite me in?" He moved her hand to his crotch and she felt his raging hard-on. "Let's fuck," he murmured.

Paul was one of the few guys she'd enjoyed having sex with, but right now the thought left her empty. "Not tonight." She tried to back away, but he placed his hands on her buttocks and jerked her tight against him, causing her short skirt to ride up her ass. The odor of beer and stale breath nearly made her gag as he moved his mouth closer to her.

Kara frowned, placed her hands against his chest, and tried to push him away. "I said not tonight, and I meant it."

"You want it," he insisted, backing her against the door at the same time he reached for the doorknob. "You need a good fucking."

"Damn it, Paul." Kara tried to push him off again, but he had her pinned too tightly. She was sure he wouldn't force himself on her, but he was majorly pissing her off. "I said no."

A sudden glow haloed Paul's hair as his lips neared hers. "Come on, babe, let's—" His words were cut short. He was there and then he wasn't, as if he'd been suddenly ripped away from her.

Kara stumbled forward with the movement and barely kept herself from falling when she saw what had happened. A tall and intimidating man held Paul by the scruff of his neck.

The man scowled and said in a voice that reverberated through the night, "Touch Kara again and I will slice your dick off at the balls."

Kara's jaw dropped as she stared at the man who'd just peeled Paul off of her.

It was Adan, the man from her dreams.

The man who'd invaded her home last night.

Chapter Two

"What the fuck—" Paul was saying as he struggled to free himself from the man who held him at arm's length.

Adan. The name rolled around in Kara's head as she stared at the tall and angry-looking warrior-god. *He's real.* From the nearly waist-length dark hair to the sword hilt glinting from its sheath. The man was real.

And what was even stranger was that she felt relief and excitement at seeing him, rather than fear, and her body went on full sexual alert. For cripe's sake, this was the man who'd broken into her home last night. What was wrong with her?

Adan tossed Paul onto Kara's front lawn, a look of distaste on his dark features. Paul landed on his ass with a thump, then scrambled to his feet, his gaze darting from Kara to Adan.

Paul seemed to come to his senses as he brushed his sandy hair out of his eyes. "Do you know this asshole, Kara? Are you going to be all right?"

Adan growled.

Kara raised an eyebrow at Paul. Even though she was confident he wouldn't have raped her, she wasn't in the mood for him. He had royally pissed her off by not taking the hint the first time. "Good night, Paul."

Even in the pale glow of the streetlight, she could see him flush. "Whatever," he said and gave her a brush-off wave as he turned away.

"Stay away from Kara," Adan said in a low rumble to Paul's back.

Paul's "Fuck off" rang clear through the night as he got to his Porsche, but he didn't look back. Kara saw Adan clench his fists and his jaw and she knew only a fine rein on his control held him back from kicking Paul's ass.

"That went well." Kara watched Paul drive off, the wheels of his sports car screeching before it shot into the night.

When the street was quiet again, she turned her gaze back to the giant of a man standing just feet from her. He had his intense eyes focused on her again, and she felt another flush of desire from her nipples to her pussy.

Now that she was alone with Adan again, she wasn't so sure she was safe, yet she still felt no fear. Now she remembered everything from last night. From the time she watched him appear on the sidewalk until he'd put his hand to her forehead and made her fall asleep. How had he done that?

"Thanks," she finally said. But then her lips twisted into a frown. "Why are you back? What do you want with me?"

Adan stepped within inches of her and she found herself backing up against the door again. Hell, he was tall. She was wearing her highest heels, yet he towered over her.

He stopped and came no closer and murmured in that unusual accent, "I do not understand it, but I am drawn to you, Kara Marks."

She didn't understand it, either, but right now she wanted to jump his bones. Everything about him attracted her, from the fire in his eyes to his long hair that flowed over his shoulders and down his back. He had an aura of power about him, yet gentleness, too. And damn, but he smelled good.

"I'm losing it." Kara sighed and shook her head. "Come in and we'll talk." She turned her back to him as she slipped the keys out of the lock and dropped them into her purse.

The last thing Adan wanted to do was talk, but he gratefully followed Kara into her home and shut the door behind him. The beautiful woman looked nervous yet confident all at once. She flicked on the lights then raised her chin and led him from the door into the finely decorated living room. She headed through the arched entryway into the kitchen, her heels clicking along the tile. He didn't know why the sword had drawn him to her again, or why he couldn't stay away. He just knew he had to be near her.

"Why did I remember you when I saw you, but not before?" she asked as she walked.

"I used thoughtpower to unlock your memories."

She glanced over her shoulder. "What about Paul? Why did you let him remember you?"

Adan shrugged. "He did not see me appear, and I used thoughtpower to ensure that he thought me only one of your suitors."

"Talented," she murmured.

As she strolled ahead of him, he watched the sway of her hips and her honey-blonde curls brushing her shoulders. She was a beautiful creature and just the thought of being more intimate with her made him so hard he could barely breathe.

"Have a seat." She gestured toward a dining table as she tossed her purse onto a countertop and shrugged out of her leather jacket. "Would you like something to drink? How about a wine cooler?" She dumped the jacket on the counter beside the purse and eyed him. "You look more the Jack Daniels type, though."

"No." He closed the few feet between them and she gave a soft gasp as he caught her by her shoulders. "I want you."

Kara's heart pounded as she stared into his black eyes. Challenge filled his gaze as he just watched her, as if waiting for her to take the next step. His mere touch made her want him so badly her panties dampened more than they already were. "Well that's getting right to the point."

He brought his face closer to hers. "I want to know you."

She caught her breath, unsure whether to let him kiss her or to punch him in the jaw. Clearing her throat, Kara backed away and he let his palms slide down her arms to her hands. He caught her in his grip and gently squeezed.

The way he held her hands and looked at her made Kara feel as if he had decided he owned her. That same flush coursed her, a glittering sensation throughout her body, but she did her best to ignore it. She cocked her head to one side. "Well then, tell me who you are."

Frowning, he gripped her hands tighter. "Love, I have no doubt you would not believe me."

"Who the hell are you to decide what I will or won't believe?" She jerked her hands away from him and scowled. "You're definitely different. You can appear out of nowhere and you carry a sword. What's not to believe?"

"All right." Adan nodded and his look remained serious. "I am a knight from the future, nearly a thousand years from now."

Trying to absorb what he was telling her, Kara leaned back against the counter and crossed her arms tight against her chest. Okay, so he was certifiable—the guy was freaking nuts.

Yet she *had* seen him appear out of thin air...although that glow could have been an illusion.

Kara shook her head. "You can't have traveled through time. It's not possible."

He smirked, no doubt from the fact that she hadn't believed him after all. "It was not possible in your time. Not even in mine." Adan's gaze never wavered from her as he spoke. "But we now live upon a planet where the people have that capability."

"So you're telling me," she said slowly, "that you're from the future and that you live on another planet."

He nodded.

Taking a deep breath, she counted to ten and then let it out in a deep sigh as she ruffled her curls. "Jeez. Couldn't you just be some normal guy instead of Mr. Nut Case?"

"Thoughtpower did not evolve until approximately six hundred years from now." Adan held out his hand, his palm up. "Perhaps you will believe this."

Kara's knees nearly gave out as she watched her purse rise from the countertop and float toward his hand. When it landed on his hand she reached out and took it from him. It was real and solid with no strings attached.

"Okeydokey." She brought the purse tight to her chest and swallowed. "So you can pop in from the future, you have mind-powers, and you're totally hot. We're a match made in heaven."

The corner of Adan's mouth quirked into a grin and she thought she'd never seen a sexier man in her life. "And what are your powers, enchantress?"

"I'm a hell of a loan agent, a workaholic, I'm a little artsy, and I have curls like springs." She set her purse aside and her gaze returned to Adan's. "Other than that, my life is pretty dull."

"You are anything but dull, Kara Marks," he murmured and caught her chin in his hand. "Do we know one another well enough that I might kiss you now?"

Maybe the guy had another power—the power to disarm her, to make her throw reason out the window. She only hesitated a moment before placing her palms to his chest. She raised herself on her toes and brushed her lips against his. "Was that what you wanted, big guy?" she murmured, meeting his dark gaze.

With what sounded like a growl, Adan slipped his hand into her curls and drew her closer. He ran his tongue along her lower lip then gently nipped at it. Kara startled at first—she'd never had a guy bite her lip before, but she loved it.

She sighed and moved her hands up to his shoulders and into his long, thick hair. His tongue slipped into her mouth and she tasted him, drawing him deeper inside until she felt as if he possessed all of her in just that one kiss.

Desire burned through Kara from the roots of her hair to that spot between her thighs that ached for him, that needed this man she didn't even know. Somewhere in the back of her mind she realized she truly knew absolutely nothing about him, yet she wanted him so bad she could taste it. What would it be like to feel him naked against her, to feel him thrust his cock deep inside? She could feel him hard against her belly, and she wondered how he might taste if she sucked his cock.

Adan moved his hands from her shoulders, slowly caressing her arms until he reached her hips. He drew her body flush with his and kneaded her butt. Her silky skirt rose up higher and higher until his hands were on her bare ass and her thong grew even wetter.

Adan stilled as he felt bare flesh beneath his hands. He drew back from the kiss and stared down at Kara. "You are naked."

"Sort of." She smiled and twirled her finger in a lock of his hair. "I have a thong on."

"Mmmm." His smile was more than carnal. "I want to taste you."

Heat flared through her at the thought, but still she said, "It's too soon for that."

Adan slid his hands to her waist and Kara gasped as he effortlessly picked her up and set her on the countertop. The granite was cool against her bare ass and her thong pulled tight against her clit, nearly causing her to come. Her skirt rode high on her thighs, almost exposing her.

"I will not force you, love, but I believe you want me as much as I want you." He moved between her thighs and kissed her, then brought his hands to her breasts and groaned against her mouth. "You can tell me to leave and I will."

Leave? The mere thought made her want to scream, *No...no!*

To hell with getting to know him better. Kara wanted this man. What better way to get to know him anyway? She braced her hands on the countertop and arched her back so that her breasts pressed against his palms. He gave a low rumble and moved his mouth down her neck to the silky blouse she wore.

Through the fabric he pinched and pulled at her nipples, then found one with his mouth and tongue and she all but mewled with pleasure. She watched him as he suckled first one breast and then the other—no way did she want him to stop.

His eyes met hers as he pushed up her blouse and then fingered the lace of her bra. "May I?" he asked, and at that moment Kara knew she would do about anything for his mouth on her nipples, his hand in her panties.

"Yeah." Her voice was husky and she looked at him through lowered lashes. "Suck them."

Adan's eyes lit with dark fire as he pulled down her bra, causing her breasts to spill into his hands. He pressed his hips harder against her pussy, spreading her legs further apart as he licked and sucked one nipple then the next.

God that felt good. "I can't believe this is happening." She arched up higher. *And I don't want it to end.* She knew she was out of her head, but right now she just didn't care. He was good—so damn good—with his mouth and his hands.

She couldn't stop moaning and making sighs and gasps of pleasure as he kneaded her breasts while he suckled them. He rose up and cool air brushed her nipples, making them even tighter.

Placing his hot palms on her thighs, he stared at her as he slowly moved them up to where her skirt barely covered her mound. "I've tasted your sweet lips and nipples," he murmured. "I want to sample the rest of you."

Hell yes. Kara trembled at the thought. God, this was crazy—he was a complete stranger, and a futuristic one at that!

Yet she'd had one-night stands before, a couple of times with guys she barely knew—friends of friends.

"I only want what you want, Kara." He slowly stroked the inside of her thigh down to her knee and back. "I will leave if you wish it."

"Don't go," she said before she could change her mind.

Adan smiled. He knew he shouldn't be here with an Earth woman from the past, but he needed to touch her, to feel her, to taste her. All he'd been able to do was think about her since last night.

Her delicious scent filled his senses as he pushed her skirt all the way up, exposing a tiny scrap of cloth covering her pussy. He peeled it off and she helped him by raising her ass. He slipped it down over her thighs and over her high heels.

For a moment he braced his hands to either side of her hips and stared down at the beautiful woman before him. Her green eyes were wide and expressive and her full lips parted. Her blouse rode high over her pale breasts, her belly bare, her skirt around her waist, her thighs spread, and her pussy wide open to him. Her folds were swollen with desire and wet with her juices.

Adan pulled her so that her ass was at the edge of the countertop. He watched her as he knelt between her thighs and lowered his head to her pussy.

"Did you know you smell of peaches and springtime?" he asked as he lightly stroked the dark blonde curls of her mound. "It has been a long time since I've seen the spring or smelled its sweet perfume."

Kara swallowed. Her pussy tingled and throbbed as he spoke, stroking her with his skillful fingers. "Why haven't you seen the spring? Have you been in prison or something?"

He brought his finger along the side of her pussy lips, but ignored the folds. "The world in which we live, it is an ice world. There is no spring, no summer, no fall. Only winter."

She could almost feel her juices dripping onto the countertop and she squirmed. "Winter is my favorite time of year—at least when I go skiing and sledding up north."

"Then you would enjoy my world." He lowered his head and the stubble on his cheek brushed the inside of her thigh. "And I would love to have you there. To warm my bed. I would fuck you morning and night."

Kara couldn't help the tremors of desire that ran through her at the image of being this man's sex kitten. It wasn't her style, but the image of him fucking her every way 'til Sunday made her hot beyond belief. "Stop talking and get down to business before I lose my mind."

He gave a soft laugh then licked her in one long swipe of his tongue. Kara almost screamed—something she never did. She wasn't a screamer, and never would be. But she'd never been so hot for a man in all her years, and had never experienced anything as erotic as this moment. He slipped a finger into her channel and she watched the big man lick and suck her pussy while finger-fucking her.

"You're good." She pressed herself tighter against his face. "So frigging *good*."

Like a big bear, Adan rumbled and continued to devour her pussy. His stubble chafed her pussy and the inside of her thighs, adding to the exquisite sensations. Her breathing grew deeper and her skin glistened with sweat as he drew her closer and closer to the brink. The climax built within her, expanding outward, bigger and bigger and bigger until it exploded.

Kara gave a soft cry as she climaxed with the most amazing orgasm of her life. Her body shuddered and wouldn't stop, and she swore she saw spots before her eyes. Adan gripped her hips in his hands and only pressed his face deeper into her pussy, licking her long and hard, driving her from one powerful orgasm to another, making her body shudder with the power of the sensations. He kept going until she'd had too many orgasms to count, until she begged him to stop.

When he finally rose up to stand between her thighs, he gathered her into his arms and held her so close to him she could hear his rapid heartbeat. She was still sitting on the countertop, his firm cock tight against her pussy. She could feel it through the material and she couldn't wait to have that cock driving in and out of her.

"Damn." Kara tilted her head to look up at Adan. "All I can say is *damn* that was great."

"You taste delicious." Adan lowered his face to hers and she caught her scent mingled with his masculine smell of winter breezes and testosterone. He kissed her then and she tasted herself on his lips, his mouth, his tongue.

"If you don't mind me asking," she murmured when he pulled away, "do they have sexually transmitted diseases in the future?"

He shook his head. "Not for centuries." He caressed her cheek and smiled. "Thank you, Kara."

She frowned, confused at the look in his eyes, as if he intended to leave. "Aren't you going to fuck me now?"

He shook his head, his long hair brushing his shoulders. "I cannot risk impregnating you, or changing the course of time."

"I have a contraceptive implant." She rubbed her upper arm where the implant was. "And haven't you already meddled with time just by being here with me?"

Adan sighed. "Aye. But it would not be fair to take pleasure from you."

"Sure it is, if I'm willing to give it." Now she was getting pissed. "I don't get you."

"I cannot allow you to remember me." His hand moved toward her forehead. "As much as I would like to, I cannot fuck you."

"What? No!" She tried to pull back from his hand, but his fingers made contact with her temple. "You bast—"

The kitchen swirled around her, and she slipped away into a world of darkness.

Chapter Three

T'ni Lael swept into the Clans' well-guarded control room, her emerald green robes swishing across the floor, her features serene as always.

Scents of incense and wind swirled into the room, following the Cwen's wake. As she practically floated across the room, she pushed back her snow-sprinkled hood with one hand, and her waist-length blonde curls tumbled over her shoulders. The beautiful queen's fair skin was unblemished, unwrinkled. Yet Adan knew T'ni Lael to be over fifty years of age, although she looked as though she was in her late thirties at best.

According to the Cwen, she had been entrusted with the task of keeping the crystal safe until *L'sen*, the one time every two decades the sun was at its strongest and would pierce Blackstar's protective shielding. What she had proposed would allow the fate of this world to be changed, to return it to what it once was, a benefit to every inhabitant of the planet.

Why the Ice-Witch wished to stop them, the stars only knew. T'ni Lael said the crystal would give the Witch great powers which she would wield to conquer the Sanor and Earth survivors alike. Apparently the Witch preferred world domination over a better life for all.

When T'ni Lael came to a stop a few feet away from Adan, she gave a deep nod.

"Cwen." Adan returned with a slight bow of his head and shoulders as he greeted the Sanor queen. She had long been a friend to him, and as always he was pleased to see her. Although of late, her presence only reminded him of his task to find the crystal and that he had yet to complete it.

"Clan Leader Valnez." The Cwen's heavily accented and halting English held a hint of something he had never heard in her tone before. Perhaps concern. Maybe desperation? "I understand you had no fortune in retrieving the crystal or the treasure last eve. Did the sword at least bring you close?"

"Perhaps near it." Adan rested his hand on the sword hilt at his side, as if it might suddenly feed him the whereabouts of the crystal this very moment. "It hummed and the runes glittered, but nothing more. I will return this night and seek the pendant with all that I have."

T'ni Lael clasped her hands in front of her, and the only telltale sign of her distress was the whitening of her knuckles. "You must bring back the treasure with it."

Adan could only answer, "I will do my best."

A flicker of something passed over the Cwen's beautiful features, and at that moment he knew she was not being completely honest with him. For the first time in the ten years he had known T'ni Lael, he felt a niggling of distrust. And Adan never danced around his gut instincts. He faced them head on.

He fixed his gaze on the Cwen's green eyes, yet he saw no deceit there, despite his feelings to the contrary. "What treasure is this you speak of?" he demanded.

For a moment the Cwen remained silent as if choosing her words carefully. She finally sighed and said, "Your heart will know, Adan Valnez."

Adan gritted his teeth and clenched his hand tighter upon the sword hilt. "Why this secrecy? Do not hold information back from me. Friend or no, I will not do anything that will allow my people to come to harm."

"I understand your concern, Adan." T'ni Lael gave a slow nod of acceptance of his words. "However, the treasure must remain safe, no matter what the outcome." The Cwen's eyes became almost pleading, full of the desperation he saw in them earlier. Yet they filled with resolve, too. "Do not ask me any more. I will not allow this most precious treasure to be discovered by any but you. I cannot take the chance that our conversation will be overheard in any way."

After a moment, Adan gave a sharp nod. "As I said, I will do my best, T'ni Lael."

"That is all that I ask." The Cwen bowed and retreated from the room in a swirl of green robes and incense.

Adan threw himself in his chair and stared at the door long after the Cwen had slipped through it. He had never had reason to doubt the Sanor queen in the decade he and his people had known her. Not long after their arrival on Blackstar, T'ni Lael had greeted them and taught them much of how to survive on this harsh world. She had led him to the snow-shrouded mines, explained how the materials could be used to make buildings and machinery, and what small bounty the planet yielded.

In turn, he had visited the Sanor in the caverns below Crystal Village, a gentle, quiet people who lived on fish they cultivated in the underground pools, roots, and a small creature much like Earth's rabbits.

Once Crystal Village had been completed, Adan invited the people of Sanor to come to the surface, to live with the Clans, but they had refused. The caverns had been their home for over two decades, where they lived, loved, and died. Only the Cwen would leave the sanctuary to visit the Clans and to impart her knowledge. He continued to have fresh vegetables and fruits that had been grown in the Clans' greenhouses sent to the caverns, which they gratefully accepted.

It was not until a few months past that the Cwen had come to him and explained about the *L'sen* Crystal and how it had been a gift from an alien race over two decades ago. She explained how it would return this planet into a verdant paradise, rich with life. T'ni Lael read to him from meticulously written records painstakingly kept in a language foreign to him. But it was the collection of vids that backed what she spoke of.

More recently she had presented the Clans with the time-arch, and Adan's sword, and had taught them the use of both. These had been gifts, too, from the aliens of long ago.

When he had asked why she had not told them sooner, she had shrugged and said, "It wasn't time. If we retrieve the crystal and the treasure too soon, it could be too easily stolen by the Ice-Witch."

Adan turned to the control room's view screen and touched the surface with his finger. Instantly an image of Echna's palace flashed across the surface. An elite force of female warriors guarded the palace, their white uniforms making them almost indistinguishable from the permanent winter landscape. If he had not had plenty of experience, he would not have been able to tell one of the Ice-Witch's warriors from a snowdrift, they were camouflaged so well.

From their few years spent on the ice-laden planet, Adan and most of his people had learned how to recognize form and movement with minimal cues. Even bundled as they were from the elements, he could distinguish one member of his own colony from another just by the way the person walked, the movements of his or her head, hands, and body. It was nearly a psychic ability they had developed since living in this winter world.

Leaning back in his chair, Adan studied the female forms, the ice-ghosts, guarding Echna's palace. They stood like statues but their pale eyes constantly roved the landscape, searching for possible intruders. As sharp as the warriors were, and as powerfully as the Ice-Witch's spells warded off intruders, it was a wonder Adan's people had been able to position a spybug in close enough proximity to give him a view of the enemy's fortress.

On the view screen, immense doors to the palace opened and Adan leaned forward. A tall, stately form practically flowed from the building. Her ethereal beauty would have had his cock at full attention, if he did not know what a deadly bitch lay behind the innocent exterior. Her delicate features, heart-shaped face, pale eyes, dark pink lips, and luscious body were sure to have men crawling at her feet.

And that was exactly where she kept them.

Echna moved through her courtyard, her snow-blonde hair floating in the breeze, her fur-lined white leather clothing clinging to her curves, and her white cape scraping flagstones. Behind her strode four female warriors, each nearly as beautiful as the Ice-Witch, and just as fair in coloring. Adan's eyes narrowed as he watched them approach a round tower on the west side of the courtyard. Echna waited for one of her warriors to open the door for her, then all five vanished within its confines.

"What are you up to, snow bitch?" Adan muttered and then commanded the view screen, "Off." His staff monitored the Ice-Witch's palace, and he would replay the vids later.

Adan turned his gaze to the insulated window and he watched snowflakes gently drift from morning skies. Fortunately, when they came to this planet, Adan's people already had the tools, the capability, and the ingenuity to build structures well protected from the cold. Inside the buildings it was as warm as springtime. Outside, it was so cold it would freeze a man's balls off if he didn't have them well guarded from the elements.

Adan's thoughts drifted and returned to Kara as they had countless times since he had visited her last night. He closed his eyes and remembered her luscious scent, the taste of her pussy, the feel of her soft skin beneath his fingers, and her rigid nipples in his mouth. His cock ached with the desire to fuck her. To drive into that beautiful pussy and to spill his seed deep in her channel.

He opened his eyes and rubbed his erection through his pants, but it only made the ache worse. A vision came to mind, of Kara on her knees, her mouth around his cock, and he nearly climaxed.

"I can relieve your needs." Lilli's voice came from the doorway and Adan cut his gaze to the dark beauty who had so often served as his pleasure-partner. He rubbed his cock again, but only because he couldn't get the image of Kara out of his mind.

Lilli walked toward him, a slow seductive sway to her shapely hips, her yellow sarong draped in a soft fall from one shoulder to her feet. One arm was bare and he could see the swell of her breast and the curve of her hip. She ran her tongue along her full lower lip, painted a soft gold, and glanced at his crotch. He had no doubt she wanted to suck his cock—the woman had the mouth of a goddess. Normally the thought of thrusting into her made his loins ache, but this time, strangely enough, the idea held little appeal.

No. All he could think of was Kara and fucking her until neither of them could tell one from the other, until they were as one.

He growled in frustration. Lilli's eyes widened and she paused. "Is something wrong, Adan?" Her gaze darted from his face to his lap and back again. "Would you prefer another pleasure-partner?"

With a sigh Adan ordered his cock to take a vacation and motioned for Lilli to come to him. When she stood before him, he took her hand in his and brushed his lips across her knuckles, then met her dark gaze. "I believe Dane is in need of your company."

She bowed and slipped her hands from his, a smile touching her lips. "I will see to him at once." The ever-ready pleasure-partner padded from the room, her bare feet making a whisper of sound as she vanished through the doorway.

His thoughts immediately returned to Kara. Adan's frustration mounted as he forced himself to stop thinking about her, and to return to the task of retrieving the powercrystal. He should be there, hunting for it now, but T'ni Lael insisted he could only search for it during Earth's night hours, and that he must return come morning's light.

Supposedly something about the connection from Earth's moon to Earth and the San Francisco province made it possible to travel in the night.

Why has the sword taken me to Kara two nights in a row? Could she have the crystal? After he had put her to bed, had slid her panties back on, straightened her clothing, and covered her with a blanket, he had searched her home again, and again to no avail.

He had left her house to haunt the streets, searching with his instincts and his well-honed hunting abilities. The sword maintained a constant humming in the general area where Kara lived. He had searched the homes near her, careful to not upset any contents in the houses. It had not been easy gaining entrance into the homes. He'd had to use thoughtpower to disengage alarm systems, and once inside needed to cause occupants to have the sudden desire for sleep. Only in one case had he been caught, but he had managed to capture the panicked woman, erase her memories, and put her into a deep sleep.

Both nights he had fruitlessly searched, he remembered the Cwen's words, that he must use his heart and soul.

His scowl deepened at the thought. He had neither heart nor soul left.

* * * * *

It was Sunday night and Kara felt restless and edgy. She perched on her living room couch trying to work on loan docs that she had scattered across the coffee table, but she couldn't focus worth crap. All she could think of was the man from her dreams.

Two nights in a row, she'd dreamed of a man called Adan, but she had never met anyone by that name, and she was sure she would have remembered him if she had. How could a dream man make her so damn hot that she had woken in dire need of an orgasm? Her vibrator hadn't begun to assuage the need and her body stayed on edge. She was so freaking horny she could just about scream.

Absentmindedly, she picked up the cube from the tabletop and ran her finger along one smooth side as she gazed without seeing at the pendant within the crystal. What was completely bizarre was how the last two days she'd woken on the sofa or in her bed wearing her street clothes, with no memory of how she had gotten there. Last night she remembered Paul walking her to her door, but *nothing* after that. Had he somehow drugged her and taken advantage of her?

No, a girl would know if that had happened. She'd feel sore, and no doubt could smell the scent of their sex if he didn't use a condom, and Paul never did. She had the implant, so they hadn't had to worry about it. They'd both been vetted, so she knew she was safe with him. Anyway, Paul might be pushy, but he wasn't a rapist. And besides, she didn't remember what happened Friday night, either.

Something weird was definitely going on. *Yeah, I'm losing it. That's what it is, Marks. Too much work and no play makes Kara a wacko girl.*

With a groan, Kara set the cube back on the coffee table, next to the picture of the orphanage and her championship high school softball team. She pushed herself up from the couch, and headed the few steps into the kitchen. Her curls bounced against her bare neck as she tried to convince herself that her lack of memory of the past two nights was due to stress, exhaustion, and nothing more.

Okay, so maybe I need a vacation. A really long vacation.

She started to grab a glass from one of the oak cabinets above the counter when she paused and stared at the granite countertop. She slid her palms over the smooth surface, picturing herself practically naked and her dream man between her thighs. The ache in her pussy was almost unbearable and she pressed her legs tighter together.

Kara shook the vision off and cut her gaze to the refrigerator. Maybe she had a cucumber or a carrot. That would do the trick.

No, right now she needed to get fucked, and no cold veggie would replace the feel of a thick, warm cock in her pussy.

Kara leaned with her back against the countertop and started to slide her fingers beneath the waistband of her jeans to take care of business.

She caught movement from the corner of her eye and almost screamed. A man leaned against the arched entry into the kitchen, his arms folded across his chest, desire in his dark eyes.

It was Adan.

Just seeing him released the floodgate in her mind, allowing her to remember everything, no doubt he'd used that so-called thoughtpower ability. For a moment she stared at him, her body going from hot to cold, her emotions running the gamut from excitement and desire to outright anger.

She was fucking pissed.

"Sonofabitch." Kara marched up to him and stared up into his dark eyes. The amusement in his gaze pissed her off even more. "How dare you come here and give me the best damn orgasm of my life, and then make it so that I can't remember it or you?"

He folded his arms and kept his gaze focused on her. "Remembering me is not allowed."

"Well I can tell you exactly where to stuff that crap." She braced her hands on her hips and scowled. "Just get the hell out of my home before I make you sorry you ever came here to begin with."

"Is that what you want, Kara?" Adan's voice was low and husky as he brought his hand up and trailed one finger along her jaw. "I do not think so."

She jerked away from his touch and poked one finger at his chest, emphasizing each word as she glared up at him. "You're nothing but an arrogant, egotistical, *bastard*."

He caught her hand against his chest and the rest of her rant evaporated into nothing.

Fuck it. She wanted him.

In a movement of fury and the most intense desire of her life, Kara grabbed a handful of his long hair and yanked his head down as she pushed herself up to meet him. His mouth captured hers in a kiss just as fierce, and her head spun with the wildness of it. Their mouths engaged in a hungry battle, and all Kara knew was that this was one war she intended to win.

Adan could hardly keep up with the wild woman in his arms, could barely hold back from taking her down to the kitchen floor and fucking her until they wore a groove in the tile.

"You bastard," Kara repeated against his lips as she wrapped her arms around his neck and climbed him. She clenched her legs around his waist as she thrust her tongue into his mouth, greedy and demanding. He grabbed her ass and held her pussy tight against his aching cock. Her lips and body were so soft, so warm in his arms. Her breasts were smashed to his chest and she managed to grind her pussy even harder against his erection.

"This time you're going to fuck me," she said as she tore her lips from his and her green eyes locked on his face. "And you're not going to do that memory blocking shit again."

"I cannot—" Adan started, but she crushed her lips against his, cutting off his words and eliminating all rational thought from his mind. Damn the consequences but he had to have her.

Half-blind with lust, he carried her to the living room and took her down to the creamy white carpet, then knelt on the floor beside her. The moment he laid her on her back, she pulled her shirt over her head and tossed it aside at the same time she kicked off her shoes. Adan could not think past the moment. All that mattered was the woman who was busy unfastening her jeans and scooting them down over her hips. He had never seen a woman undress so fast in all his years.

When she was clad only in her matching bright pink thong and bra, he grabbed her hands and trapped them within his grip. "Slow down, love."

A defiant gleam lit her eyes as she tugged her hands from his. She yanked her bra cups down and beneath her breasts so that each nipple jutted up high. "Hurry up."

Adan eased to his feet but never took his eyes off of Kara—or rather her tantalizing breasts—as he pulled his tunic over his head, kicked off his boots and dropped his sword belt to the floor. When he found himself only in his pants, a flash of reason came back to his mind — he shouldn't be doing this — but the remnants of that reason vanished the moment Kara got to her knees and reached for his waistband.

So quickly it caught him off guard, she had his pants unfastened and his mighty erection in her warm hands. His brain suddenly shifted to the head of his cock and all he could think of was the way she was stroking him and how close her mouth was to him.

"Now this is what I like," she murmured, her eyelids lowered and her attention riveted to his cock. "Nice and thick and long." She flicked her tongue over the tiny opening where a drop of semen had taken shape. In the same moment she slid her fingers down to his balls and caressed them, and he practically shuddered with desire. "Mmmmm. You taste good."

She slipped her lips over his cock and lightly scraped her teeth over the sensitive skin. Adan thought he would spill his seed before he even had a chance to take his next breath.

"Damnation, woman." He watched his cock sliding in and out of her mouth as she watched him. Her naked breasts called to him and he wished he could reach them to tweak her nipples as she sucked him. Instead he groaned and slid his fingers into her wild mass of curls as she moved up and down his length, her hot mouth nearly boiling him alive. "I cannot hold back."

Her eyelids lowered and she sucked harder and lightly squeezed his balls.

Heat started in his groin and flushed outward, spreading to his buttocks, his chest and shoulders and straight to his head. Even his scalp prickled and he swore hair rose on his arms as his orgasm roared through him. He barely contained a shout as his fluid spurted into her mouth and she swallowed until the last jet of come had emptied from his cock.

When she slipped him from her mouth, she rubbed his half-erection against her bare breasts, first one nipple and then the other, spreading the moisture from her mouth over her skin.

His erection doubled in size.

"Fuck me," Kara ordered as she tugged at his cock, forcing him to go down toward the floor with her, and between her thighs. "By God, you'd better fuck me now."

Chapter Four

Kara brought Adan down between her thighs, tugging his cock to bring him toward her pussy so that he had no choice but to follow her. He was still wearing his leather pants, and she was wearing her thong, and she groaned in frustration that she needed to remove her panties.

When she was flat on her back on the plush carpeting, Adan caught her wrist and forced her to release his cock. "Slow down, love," he said as he released her. He rose up and shucked off his pants.

"Bullshit." Kara squirmed and started to force down her thong, but he stopped her again.

"I mean it." He grasped her wrists in one hand and pinned them over her head. "I will tie you up if I have to."

She shivered at the mere thought and her nipples tightened. "I dare you."

Fire flashed in his eyes. "Do not start something you are not going to win."

"Oh, I'm going to win all right." She answered his challenge by arching her breasts.

As she expected, his cock did the thinking for him. His gaze dropped to her chest and his erection bucked against her belly. In a near roar he lowered his head and caught one nipple in his mouth. Kara gasped and thrust her breasts higher as she struggled against his hold, but he kept her wrists pinned securely above her head.

Damn but he was good. He had a way of licking, sucking and lightly biting her nipples that made her crazy. Tiny orgasms rippled through her pussy just from the way he was ravaging her breasts.

"You've got to fuck me." Kara was near tears with the need to feel Adan's cock inside her. "Do it now."

"Patience." Adan released her wrists and then grasped the sides of her thong. "I haven't even begun with you."

Kara groaned. "You're going to kill me. Seriously. I'm not going to last much longer."

He tugged her underwear down at the same time he licked a path from her breasts to her belly button. His long hair flowed over her, the thick strands stroking her like fingers caressing her skin. The sensations were amazing and her pussy clenched and spasmed with another mini-orgasm.

Slowly he inched the thong down her thighs but left it around her knees as he nuzzled the curls of her mound. Kara tried to kick her underwear off the rest of the way but he stopped her, his big hands clenching her thighs so tight she couldn't move.

"My way," he murmured as he raised his head to look at her.

He really was trying to kill her.

"Fine. Take your time." She moaned as he licked the patch of hair between her thighs. She could barely speak as she added, "Just hurry up about it."

Adan dragged her thong down further while he licked a trail down the inside of one leg to the inside of her knee. Her pussy gushed with moisture, surely soaking the carpet beneath her, and she caught her own scent mingling with his masculine smell. He continued his maddening pace, easing her thong down to her feet and tracing a path along her calf to the inside of her ankle.

When he finally tossed aside the bright pink thong, Kara was ready for him to plunge into her. But instead the bastard moved to her other ankle and began kissing his way back up along the inside of that leg toward her pussy.

Demands weren't working, so Kara resorted to begging. "Adan, *please.*"

He gave a soft laugh and she was tempted to kick him.

But he finally, *finally*, reached her slit. He used his hands to part her folds and breathed deeply of her scent. It was so completely erotic watching him close his eyes and inhale the smell of her sex. His eyelids rose and his gaze met hers, and then he licked her clit.

She nearly came apart at the seams like a stuffed doll with too much padding. "Adan. *Damn.*" If only he would drive his cock into her, she would be a happy woman.

Adan seemed intent on driving her out of her mind instead. He slipped two fingers into her core and laved her folds. He never licked the same place twice. Rather, he moved around, not giving her a chance to come.

Kara gripped her hands in his hair and tugged at him. "What do I have to do to get you to fuck me?"

To her relief he moved up so that his hands were braced to either side of her shoulders and his cock against the opening to her channel. "You taste incredible," he said, and dipped his mouth down to kiss her. Oh, man, but he could kiss. She loved the taste of him mingled with her own, loved the smell of his skin and the winter breeze scent of his hair.

"If you don't take me now," she said when he pulled away from the kiss, "next time you come near me I'm going to throw something at you."

The corner of his mouth curved into a wicked grin as he brought his hand to his cock and held it against her opening. "You are one fiery little wench."

Just as she thought he was going to tease her some more, he drove his cock deep inside her pussy.

Kara cried out, her eyes widening in surprise. Adan stretched her, filled her, like no other man had before. He held still, the expression on his face telling her that it pained him to hold himself back, and it pleased her that she affected him as much as he affected her.

A fine coating of sweat broke out over her skin and she moved her hips, trying to get him to move, to really fuck her. Slowly Adan pumped in and out of her pussy, his cock bringing her to the brink then pulling her back again. Mini-orgasms rippled through her and she knew she was well on the way to the mother of all climaxes.

He began to drive into her harder and harder, faster and faster, causing more orgasms to spasm her pussy around his cock.

Kara went wild beneath him. She rammed her hips up to meet every thrust and raked her nails down his powerful back. He growled and it seemed to fuel him on. She raised her head up to meet his and their mouths, tongues, and lips met in a kiss that made her head spin. Everything spiraled out of control. God, she had never been fucked like this, never been so crazy for a man that she didn't know up from down or where his body began and hers ended.

The next thing she knew they were rolling across the plush carpet and she found herself on top of him and then beneath him again. His cock never left her pussy and his mouth never left hers. They were so out of control with one another that her head wouldn't stop spinning. Their bodies were slick with sweat, their breathing labored, and her face burned from the way his stubble chafed her skin.

They rolled across the floor again and smashed into a piece of furniture. A loud crash echoed through the living room, followed by the sound of breaking glass, but Kara could care less what had shattered.

He broke the kiss and they both gasped for air. His gaze was feral and his mouth cut into a fierce expression. They bucked against each other as he braced himself above her and continued to fuck her.

Kara caught her breath as her body seized. It was like a powerful hand gripped her entire body and squeezed it in its warm grip. A hand that sensitized every nerve ending in her body from her toes to her ass to her pussy and her nipples. And then her orgasm ripped through her with the force of a lightning storm. Bright flashes exploded in her mind and a strangled cry tore from her lips.

Adan kept fucking her, drawing her orgasm out into one continuous climax that wouldn't let her go. Every jerk of her body, every thrust of his hips made it stretch out until she thought it was possible to die from too much pleasure.

When she was sure she couldn't take one second more, Adan shouted and pressed his hips tight against her pussy. She could feel the pulse and throb of his cock inside her, the power of his orgasm surely as intense as her own.

With a groan, Adan rolled onto his back, keeping his cock within Kara's core. She found herself on top of him, captured tight against his chest. They were both hot and sweaty, and the smell of their sex was so strong she was sure it filled the room. Her ear was pressed to his chest, his heartbeat loud and fast beneath her ear.

She was so sated she could barely keep her eyes open. "You'd better not make me forget you," she murmured as exhaustion overcame her. "I'll never fuck you again if you do."

Adan had never known anyone like Kara before. No woman had made him so crazy with lust that he had forgotten anything and everything but her.

He watched as her eyelids drifted shut and her breathing became deep and even. Something in his chest warmed and he felt protective and caring for this creature who had captivated him so completely.

Damnation. Adan scrubbed his hand over his face and scowled. What in the stars' names had he been thinking? Obviously he had not been thinking with anything but his cock. He could not have developed feelings for this woman. He would not. After his losses, with the duty and responsibilities of Clan leader, he had nothing to offer her.

Carefully he slipped his cock out of her channel and shifted so that she was on the carpet and he was on his knees. For a moment he simply looked down at the beautiful sleeping woman and his heart clenched. She looked so peaceful, so thoroughly satisfied. She smelled of his come and her juices, along with her sweet scent of peaches and springtime. Her skin was still coated in a fine covering of sweat and her pussy glistened with moisture.

With a growl he scooped Kara into his arms and stood, then headed into her bedroom. He settled her on her bed and she murmured in her sleep, something that sounded like "Adan" and "so damn good".

All she had on was her bra, and he removed it just to make her more comfortable. After covering her with a blanket, he stood over her and rubbed his hand over his face again. *Damn.* He had broken rules and now felt affection for this Earth woman of the past. And in good conscience, he could not make her forget him. He had to allow her to keep her memories of their time together, which could foul up the timeline in ways he could scarcely imagine.

Furious with himself, he strode back into the living room and yanked his clothes back on in quick, angry jerks. When he strapped on his sword, he paused. The humming was louder this time, and the weapon practically trembled.

His pulse rate picked up and he gripped the hilt and withdrew the sword. The runes glittered brighter than ever. Somewhere near — the crystal was closer than ever. But where?

For the third time Adan searched Kara's home from attic to basement, this time going through everything including her kitchen drawers, her refrigerator, and every place imaginable. He even carefully stepped around the shattered glass on the living room floor and searched her couch cushions. He thought about cleaning up the mess, but by the time he had finished searching the rest of the house, it was close to dawn and he was not sure what she would want to do with the fragments of her broken item. Throughout his search the sword maintained its constant humming, and the runes continued to glow, but it never grew any louder, never gave any other indication that he was close.

When he could wait no longer to return to Blackstar, he gripped the hilt of his sword and closed his eyes. Using all his thoughtpower, he matched the sword's energy to the time-arch and felt the familiar grinding sensation in his body. He gritted his teeth. Earth released its hold and Adan shot back through time and space to Blackstar.

* * * * *

Fall sunlight caressed Kara's face and she snuggled deeper into her covers, feeling that incredible feeling that came from good sex and being thoroughly satisfied.

Kara bolted up in bed, three thoughts jamming at her brain at once.

She was late for work.

Adan had fucked her last night.

She remembered everything.

The far more important realization grabbed her and images flashed through her mind. She remembered him, remembered *everything*. Her body felt sore and well-used, and she was sure she had a bruise on her hip from where they had crashed into a piece of furniture.

Oh. My. God. Kara twirled her finger in her hair as she stared at a mural on her bedroom wall, seeing only the vivid memories in her mind. She had just had the most unbelievable sex of her life, and it had been with a man who claimed to be from the future. Just the thought of the wildness of their passion made warmth swell from her pussy to her belly.

Wincing from the pain of the bruise on her hip, Kara climbed out of bed and headed for the shower. She smelled of sex, felt sticky from dried sweat, come, and her own juices, and her body ached from the incredible workout it had received.

She'd never felt better or happier in her life.

Kara switched the shower on and frowned at her thoughts. Happy about what? A great fuck? Or that she'd met someone that she could easily fall for...

Great. She lusted after, and was starting to develop feelings for a man who had broken into her house, had the ability to mess with her mind and cause her to her forget him, and a guy she might not even see again. How did a girl call a guy from another planet and from the future, anyway?

Earth to Future Boy, long distance call for you.

She stepped under the warm spray and soaped her body with her favorite bath gel. It did make her smell of spring and peaches, just like Adan had said.

When she finished showering and dressing, Kara called in sick to work and then set about straightening her living room. Even the couch cushions were out of place. But what did she care? She'd just had the world's best sex. Hey, best interplanetary sex if what Adan said was true.

When she reached the coffee table, she saw what had broken. The glass on her softball team picture was smashed, and the cube containing the pendant was cracked. At least the picture of her and the kids at the orphanage had made it.

She glared at the cube and the smashed glass. "Well that sucks."

Although she wasn't sure of the strange appeal of the cube. She should just toss it. The thing had always reminded her of how she'd never had a family to call her own. Never had parents who loved her, cared for her.

Shaking the thoughts away, she settled on her knees to clean up the mess. A spider web of fractures made the cube so milky-white she couldn't see her pendant. She pushed aside the broken team picture and picked up the cube, careful not to cut herself on a fragment or a fracture. When she held it, the cube heated in her hands and she almost dropped it.

It began to melt.

Kara's eyes widened and her heart pounded in her throat. The cube was melting before her eyes, like ice on a summer's day.

It fell into two partially melted pieces. The pendant and its silver chain dropped into her lap.

Heart still pounding, Kara set the melted halves of the cube on the coffee table, but her attention was completely on the pendant that was in her lap. It was as if it was some kind of magnet and she couldn't force her attention or her thoughts away from it. The crystal, about two inches in length, looked more like a phallic symbol than ever. It was still bordered with silver, but it was different now. Instead of an iridescent white, the crystal was black with bits of silver in it—and the silver actually appeared to be swirling.

She blinked. "Kara Marks, you've done lost it. First Mr. Future Fuck and now you're hallucinating."

She picked up the pendant from her lap and nearly dropped it again. The crystal felt almost hot to the touch and she swore it vibrated in her hand. Her belly flip-flopped and hair stood up on her nape. Something very strange was going on.

Yeah. I'm losing my mind.

Before she even realized what she was doing, Kara took the pendant by the chain and slipped it over her head. The crystal rested between her breasts and she felt warmth spread from it, throughout her body. All soreness from her wild night with Adan slowly dissipated. Her body felt beyond invigorated. Tingling sensations traveled from her head to her toes and she had the sudden desire to dance and laugh and sing.

And fuck. She really needed *another* good fuck.

Her pussy and nipples felt the same tingling, only magnified beyond belief. She was sure she was going to come just from what the pendant was doing to her body.

"You've lost it, Marks." Kara stroked the crystal with one finger and an almost electrical feeling traveled from her hand throughout the rest of her body. "You've definitely lost it."

Chapter Five

Goddamn it, I fucked her. Adan paced the travel chamber and raked his hand through his hair. *I actually fucked her.* Ever since last night he couldn't get his mind off Kara. Instead of relieving the ache in his cock, it had only made him desire her a thousand times more. He could still smell her rich, womanly scent, could still taste her upon his tongue.

But he had done more than take her. He had opened up a part of him that he had attempted to kill off long ago. When his wife and his child had died in the final battle at the end of the Age of Sorcery, he had been certain he would never love again. He had loved them both so much that even after a decade his heart still ached at the memory, and he knew it always would.

Somehow there was a part of him that realized he could easily love Kara just as much. He barely knew her, yet it was as if he had known her forever. In another lifetime perhaps. Her spunk, with an edge of vulnerability, made him want to hold her close, made him want to know more about her, made him want to be with her always.

"Something is disturbing you, my friend," came Dominik's voice from behind him.

Adan turned his scowl on Dominik and Dane, who stood in the travel chamber's entryway. "Nothing but the powercrystal concerns me."

Dane's eyebrows drew close. "I do not like being lied to. Tell us the truth—all of the truth. There is more than you have been telling us."

With a roar of frustration, Adan rounded on Dane. "Do not presume to question me, friend. *Your* concern is to man the controls while I retrieve the crystal and return it to the Cwen."

In a couple of strides the knight reached Adan, but Dominik moved between the two. It always amazed Adan how quickly Dominik could appear wherever he chose to.

"Enough." Dominik raised his hands in a gesture of truce. "This does nothing to solve our dilemma."

With a growl, Dane moved to the conference table, threw himself into a chair and folded his arms across his chest. "Adan would be well advised to be truthful, else risk all our lives and the crystal."

"I have told you all that concerns you and our mission." Adan glared at his friend.

The knight steadily eyed Adan as if measuring him up. "What did you learn about the *L'sen* Crystal's whereabouts?"

Adan gave another sigh of frustration. "Only that it is in the Old San Francisco area of that age. I felt its pull, but something muffled its power."

Dane clenched his fist on the polished tabletop. "If only we could accompany you. Three would be better than one to search for the damnable crystal."

"Aye. But our only choice," Adan said as he moved away from the table and toward the time-arch, "is for me to continue to return to Old Earth during its night when the signal is the clearest."

"What about the Ice-Witch's warriors?" Dominik gestured west, in the general direction of Echna's realm. "How do we know the ice-ghosts are not closing in on the crystal? Or that they have not already found it?"

"We do not." Adan's frustration mounted as he acknowledged to himself that he had to stay away from Kara this night. She was too much of a distraction and he needed to be out searching.

Dominik moved to the control panel. "You had best be on your way."

Silently, Adan strode up to the time-arch and paused. His expression was grim and he gave one last scowl at Dane.

When he stepped up and stood within the time-arch's confines, he held his hand on his sword hilt. Instantly an electric shock jolted him and the blade hummed. He withdrew it and the runes fairly flamed upon the blade.

The crystal.

He felt its call, strong and sure. He mentally reached out for it and at the same time he felt a pull toward Kara. His gut and his heart told him all he needed to know.

Kara had the crystal. And she was in trouble.

* * * * *

Tugging at the curl over her forehead, Kara studied her living room with an appraising eye. It damn near sparkled now, as did the rest of her house, and the smells of pine cleaner and floral carpet freshener caused her to wrinkle her nose.

The entire day Kara had dealt with a sense of nervousness, an anxiety that kept her on edge. She had cleaned her house obsessively from top to bottom, attic to basement.

And she had never stopped thinking about Adan and their wild night together. Would he come back tonight? Or would she never see him again? She could still feel his hands upon her body, his cock sliding deep inside her pussy.

The whole day through the crystal had burned where it lay upon her chest. A kind of heat that filled her body with warmth and energy. It felt right and she couldn't imagine going without it, ever again.

What was with this crystal, and why didn't she want to take it off?

Kara sighed and released the curl so that it sprang back against her forehead. She had so much energy she was sure she could run around the block at least a dozen times and still not be tired. She should go to the orphanage like she'd been planning to, and spend time with the children. Or perhaps call Sheri or Jan and chat about nothing. Yet she didn't want to talk with anyone or leave the house for any reason. It was as if she *couldn't*.

She groaned and moved to the bay window. She had too much excess energy to sit down, but she stared out into the gathering darkness while she absently fondled the pendant nestled between her breasts. With the coming of night, the crystal made her feel even more jittery, more anxious than before.

What's with you, Marks?

The feeling intensified, and Kara rubbed her palms up and down her faded jeans. Even her sexual energy magnified and she thought she would scream in frustration. Her nipples ached for Adan's touch and her panties remained in a constant state of dampness.

Outside a car passed by, then another, and then the street quieted again. Kara turned away from the window and headed into the kitchen to fix herself a sandwich. When she opened the fridge, she just stared at the contents, not seeing anything at all. Cool air from the fridge brushed over her body and her nipples tightened. Damn that pendant, all she could think about was sex.

All she wanted was Adan.

She knew it had to be purely sexual, because she didn't know him that well. Hell, she really didn't know him at all. He was intense, single-minded, and powerful, yet she was aware of something more about him. His caring, his moral code. She could see it in those dark eyes. But those same eyes seemed to be holding back, hiding something from her.

What did she know? She'd only met the man three times.

An icy-cold breeze sailed through her house, causing her hair to rise from her shoulders and her button-up blouse to flatten against her breasts. The breeze carried the scent of peppermint and her nipples tightened from the chill.

Kara straightened and let the fridge door slowly close. "Adan?" She could barely keep herself from running to the hallway, knowing that it had to be him.

She rounded the corner from the kitchen to the hall and came to an abrupt stop.

Four women with white fur-lined hoods and capes were striding toward her, their white boots soundless against the tiles, as if they were ghosts. Their pale eyes almost vanished against their translucent skin, and their expressions were intense and focused upon Kara. Behind them the front door was closed, yet the chill wind continued to blow through her house, and their white-blonde hair whipped across their faces.

And they each carried large swords with curved blades.

Kara backed up toward the kitchen, her heart pounding against her ribcage. She needed to dial 911 or grab a knife to defend herself, but neither her phone nor the knife drawer was close enough. Something about the look upon their faces scared her more than Adan had the first time he had appeared in her home.

"What—" Kara said as the women came to a stop in front of her. "What are you doing in my home?" she asked as she stepped back from them again.

The women stared at Kara's chest and she realized the crystal was burning even hotter than before. She followed their gazes and glanced down to see that the black crystal was practically glowing silver with the flecks swirling throughout it.

Kara's gaze tore from the pendant to the women, only to find the four now surrounding her. They moved as silently as spirits and Kara wondered if she might be dreaming.

"She is the one," said the woman closest, but the words did not come from her lips. Instead it came from a small box-shaped pendant at her throat. "She bears the crystal."

Kara forced herself to stop staring at the woman's throat. She raised her chin and clenched her hands at her sides. A chill skittered down her backside at the thought of the wicked blades of the women who now stood to her sides and behind her. "Just get out of my house before I call the cops."

"Secka." A woman with a small pale mole on her cheek and a box pendant at her throat nodded toward the one who had first spoken. "Perhaps we should behead this one and take the crystal to Echna."

A sick feeling weighted Kara's stomach at the thought and she nearly screamed.

The one called Secka shook her head. "No, Chai. The Ice-Witch wants her unharmed."

What in the hell are they talking about?

Kara thought about going for Secka, the woman who appeared to be the leader. But in the next moment she felt the point of a blade in her back and she went completely still.

Oh, shit.

"Do not move." Secka and another woman grabbed Kara's arms, their grips so tight they were bound to leave bruises. She felt the rush of ice-cold air even harsher than before. Everything around her blurred as if she was in a snow globe, white particles whirling around her.

As the world faded she could have sworn she heard Adan's roar of fury.

Fire burned through Adan as he rushed the women who surrounded Kara, his blade held high. He was prepared to battle all four skilled warriors to reach his woman, to save her and the crystal.

White flakes whipped around Kara and two of the ice-ghosts.

They vanished.

Adan stopped in his tracks. In that split second his thoughts ran through every scenario, every possible way to save his woman.

He lowered his arm, leaving his sword resting at his side. There were no other options. Only one choice remained for him now, only one way to save Kara.

The remaining two ghost-warriors stepped forward, each with her curved blade held at the ready. Adan surrendered his sword to one ice-ghost as the other grasped his arm in her icy hand.

* * * * *

Kara slammed to her hands and knees on a cold and unforgiving surface. Her head still spun but the swirling white began to slow around her until it vanished like dandelion fluff on the wind. Vaguely she was aware of the two women in white stepping away.

Her breathing was hard and heavy as she stared down at the white surface she had landed upon, her pendant swinging from her neck. Her mind couldn't quite process what had just happened. Perhaps she was dreaming—

"So you are the bearer of the *L'sen*." An icy voice rang through the chill air and Kara slowly raised her head to see that she was essentially groveling before a beautiful woman perched upon a white throne. The woman wore a white bodysuit beneath matching fur-lined robes, and her eyes were the same pale shade of snow as the women who had captured Kara.

Gingerly Kara pushed herself to her feet, pain shooting through her knees as she stood. The pendant fell against her chest, its heat warming her despite the cold in the room, and some of her aches vanished. In a daze, she glanced at her surroundings to see she was in a beautiful room with glittering white walls.

The walls are made of sculpted ice. I'm in an ice palace, with an ice queen.

When Kara's gaze returned to the woman perched on the ice-carved throne, the woman smiled. The expression chilled Kara deep in her gut. If she hadn't met Adan, if he hadn't let her remember — if she hadn't believed his story about being from the future — she would have lost her mind from shock and fear. As it was, she was nervous, frustrated, and full of awe.

"Welcome home, Kara of Sanor," the woman said with a slight nod of her head.

Kara raised her chin. "I don't know what the hell you're talking about, but you'd better take me back home."

The woman laughed, the sound crisp and clear like ice tinkling in a crystal goblet. "I am Echna." She waved her hand as if to encompass the room, or perhaps the entire building around them. "This is your new home."

Kara narrowed her eyes and ignored the hand. "I don't *think* so."

The woman who called herself Echna raised one pale eyebrow and relaxed back in her throne. "So long as you bear the *L'sen*, you will be my guest."

"I don't know what planet you think you've landed on," Kara said, biting out each word, "but you can't tell me what to do. And you can't hold me here against my will."

Echna's eyes glowed an eerie white as she held her hand up, palm facing down, and then slowly lowered it. In the next instant, Kara felt a force so powerful that she dropped to her already-throbbing knees, landing hard on the ruthless ice floor. She barely choked back a cry as pain lanced her joints again.

Her pendant burned hot against her chest. Heat rushed over her body, as if she could burst into a ball of flame and melt everything around her.

Echna's gaze dropped to Kara's pendant, but her only reaction was a slight twitch along her jaw. Her unreadable, colorless stare returned to Kara's face.

"I will not allow you to destroy our way of life." Echna's eyes glowed even whiter than before. "Remove the crystal."

Kara tried to get to her feet again, but a force continued to hold her down. Another few minutes, and her knees would freeze just like the sculpted walls.

"Like hell I'll give it to you." Not only had it been a gift from her parents, even if they had abandoned her, but something told her it would be a bad idea to hand over the crystal to this weird Echna creature.

Kara expected the women on each side of her to hold her down and yank off the crystal, but neither of them moved.

The woman pushed herself out of her throne and strode to where Kara was being held to a kneeling position by the invisible force.

Echna bent over Kara and the silk of her long white-blonde hair brushed over Kara's cheeks. The scent of peppermint was strong as Echna leaned forward, then brushed her lips over Kara's.

Kara was so taken by surprise that her jaw dropped. Warmth seemed to flow from her to Echna, as if the woman was drawing heat from her body. An electric jolt jerked through Kara. Stars flashed before her eyes and she felt herself falling, falling, and being caught against a soft form. She fought to keep her eyes open, to stay awake, but the draw was too powerful. Her energy stolen, she slipped into darkness.

✷ ✷ ✷ ✷ ✷

Adan gritted his teeth as the ghost-warriors bore him away to the Ice-Witch's realm. Swirling white frost blinded his eyes and stung his face. It smelled of winter and peppermint, and felt like a powerful snowstorm.

When they finally stopped, Adan barely kept to his feet. He swayed, his head still whirling with the white flakes that vanished in moments.

They had arrived in a small white chamber. The ice-ghosts released him immediately and backed up with their blades in attack position. From his spying, Adan knew the women could wield their weapons as the finest of warriors. Their curved swords, as well as his own, gleamed in the light coming from a skylight in the roof, in the otherwise lightless, doorless, windowless chamber.

The warrior with a pale mole on her cheek tilted her head and studied Adan. Her words came through the translation module at her throat as she said, "Is he not a fine specimen, Tanon?"

"Indeed." The other warrior gave a soft laugh and motioned to him with his own sword. "He would be a fine addition to our stable. Our men would be jealous, but he would be worth it."

The moled one smiled. "Yes, he would make the finest of concubines."

Adan balanced on the balls of his feet, hoping the women would come at him. He was confident that no matter their skill he could best these two ice-ghosts, even though he had no weapon of his own.

Instead the woman called Tanon slipped her hand into a pocket of her jumpsuit and extracted what looked like a small icicle. She tossed it in front of Adan, and it rolled and hit the toe of his boot. Immediately the intense smell of peppermint hit him full force. His head ached and his eyes watered.

The warriors gave each other a grin then watched him. "He would be a fine male to enjoy pleasures with," said Tanon.

Adan took a step toward the women. His knees buckled. He pitched forward and slammed against the icy cold floor.

Fucking ice-bitches, he tried to say, but his mouth was as paralyzed as his body.

Helpless and completely unable to move, Adan could only lay there while the ice-ghosts stripped him of his clothing. He fought the magic of the icicle with everything he had, but could do nothing.

When he was entirely naked, the women rolled him onto his back. Tanon tapped her hand on the cold, cold floor, and a crystal-clear loop rose up from the surface, beside his neck. A collar and chains made of white links were attached to the loop.

Again Adan struggled to move, but his body remained as frozen as the intense expressions on the faces of his captors.

Tanon clamped the collar around Adan's neck, the chain rattling against the floor as she moved. "Do you not think we should sample him, Chai?"

The other woman gave a soft laugh. "I wish, dear sister."

When the ice-bitch finished, she glanced up at Chai and smiled. "I like this one." Tanon settled on one knee beside Adan. She trailed her finger down his abdomen to his flaccid member. "Impressive, even when not aroused." A devious look crossed her perfect features as she lowered her head and her mouth near his cock.

"The Ice-Witch will not approve," Chai warned in a tone that held a certain amount of nervousness.

Tanon laughed and slid her tongue down the length of Adan's staff.

It was apparently the only part of his body *not* frozen.

The traitorous appendage grew larger with every stroke of Tanon's tongue, and all Adan could do was lie there and watch his cock rise like the mast of a sailship.

When Tanon reached the tip of his erection, she licked the pearl of his semen and gave a small moan. "I want this man."

Chai gave a nervous glance around the doorless room. "You don't have time. The Ice-Witch knows we're back. She will be here any moment."

"I could take him fast." Tanon ran her hand along Adan's cock. "And I could take him hard."

"But you will not take him at all."

At the sound of the Ice-Witch's voice, Tanon scrambled to her feet. Chai straightened and turned to the witch who had appeared in the chamber. Flecks of snow still swirled around the woman before slowly vanishing.

"My apologies, lady." Tanon bowed her head.

"I did not give you leave to touch our *guest.*" Echna gave a wave of her hand in Tanon's direction. "Back to your post."

Tanon visibly swallowed and bowed again. "Yes, lady." She kept her eyes lowered as she moved to one wall. She raised her hand, palm facing the wall, and moved it in a slow circle. Adan watched with intense concentration as a large crystal-clear bubble formed where the wall had been. Tanon stepped into the bubble and then the ice-wall melded behind her, whole once again.

"Give me his sword," Echna ordered Chai, who instantly obeyed. Echna flicked her fingers in the direction Tanon had departed. "Leave us."

Chai quickly left the same way Tanon had.

The Ice-Witch slowly walked around Adan, until she had completely circled him. "So," she said, "Here lies the great Clan Leader, Adan Valnez."

Adan wished he could move. He would throttle the bitch.

Echna pursed her lips and tapped one finger on her chin. "Now that I have the crystal, your sword, the woman and you, my people are almost safe."

Frozen into immobility, Adan could only watch as she vanished the same way she had come.

Chapter Six

In a haze that took a moment to clear, Kara woke on a soft pad. She blinked away the remnants of fog and came to a sudden realization. Her clothes were gone and she was freezing her ass off.

The smell of peppermint and winter air filled her senses. Memories—or perhaps dreams—battered her mind. She remembered women appearing in her home, being caught up in a blizzard, meeting some woman called Echna. And that woman had kissed her and made her pass out. What the hell was going on?

It all had to be a dream, a very bad dream.

Yet she knew it wasn't, no matter how hard she tried to fight the truth.

"She wakes, Daar," came a woman's voice from behind her, and she recognized it as Secka's, the woman who had been the leader when she was kidnapped.

The two women moved within Kara's sight. The one called Daar smiled, and from that small box at her throat came, "Isn't she lovely?" Despite the fact that her comments projected from the box pendant, her words spilled out in a clear and beautiful voice, as if she was speaking through her lips.

Instead of answering, Secka moved to Kara's side. "Rise," she said.

Kara was completely exposed and vulnerable to these women who had kidnapped her, and she had no choice but to obey. She found she was in a smaller room now, devoid of anything but the mat. The floor and ceiling were the usual white and the walls also looked like they had been carved from ice.

"Where are my clothes?" Kara demanded when she had pushed herself to a sitting position on the floor mat.

"It is only to ensure you will not attempt to leave us." Secka reached for Kara's arm and carelessly brushed one gloved hand against her nipple.

A bolt of sensation traveled through Kara and she caught her breath in surprise. The pendant burned against her chest, and the sexual ache between her thighs became more intense than ever. Heat flushed through her—she couldn't believe that such desire could come from a woman's touch—and she bit her lip hard to fight away the sensations.

Each woman took Kara by an arm and brought her to her feet, then forced her to walk through an open doorway. Her aching knees threatened to give out on her, but she managed to keep up with the strides of the two women. Their leather clothing brushed her bare body and the air chilled her skin.

Completely bewildered and pissed off, Kara allowed herself to be escorted from the room without protest. The blades Secka and the other woman carried were enough of a reminder that she was in deep shit. Not to mention she had absolutely nothing on.

Even stranger was the phallic-looking pendant lying between her naked breasts. Beside the fact that it made her hot and horny beyond belief, it comforted her. It made her feel safe despite being held captive by ghostly pale women with knives. Big knives.

The two women strode on either side of Kara, each with a firm grip on her arms. Kara attempted to memorize the layout of tunnels, but it was hopeless. There was little of notice, and they went up and down so many passageways that she was sure she wouldn't be able to find her way out even if she had a map. She had an incredible memory for names and faces, but directions were another story.

Opaque white walls curved and rounded overhead. The ever-present chill caused Kara's teeth to chatter and goose bumps to prickle her skin, not to mention making her nipples as hard as ice chips. She still had a hard time believing what was happening to her. Could she be in some kind of coma, dreaming everything?

It was all far too real.

While they walked, Daar pressed a button at the side of the box at her throat. She spoke, this time through her lips. It sounded like a command, but Kara couldn't understand the language that emerged. It was unlike anything Kara had ever heard before.

When Daar finished, Kara scowled up at her. "Can you give me some kind of clue as to what's going on here?" Kara's voice echoed through the hallway, bouncing from ice wall to ice wall. "You forced yourselves into my house, kidnapped me, and took all my clothes. The least you can do is tell me why."

Secka turned her pale gaze on Kara. "You are the one. You bear the pendant," she said, as though that should answer everything.

"You've definitely got me confused with someone else." Kara slipped on a slick patch on the floor, but the two women easily held her up and continued walking.

They finally came to stop before a blank wall. Secka kept a tight hold on Kara's arm with one hand while she waved her free hand in a slow circle, palm facing the wall.

The wall bowed toward them and then turned clear. A giant crystal bubble appeared where the solid wall had been. Too startled to even think straight, Kara stumbled when a pair of hands pushed her forward, into the bubble.

Immediately, she felt like her naked body was wrapped in a cocoon of snow. She couldn't see, couldn't breathe and was freezing her nipples off. She barely kept from tripping over her own bare feet as she burst from the bubble into a small room.

She felt the presence of the two women following behind, but her gaze was riveted on the sight before her.

Adan was spread-eagled on the floor, a collar around his neck. His glorious body was as naked as hers, and the room was empty save for her lover. Adan didn't move or make a sound. But his eyes—they were black flames that promised retribution.

For a long moment, Kara couldn't tear her gaze from Adan's. She saw the fury in his eyes, but his concern for her, too.

She ran to his side and dropped to her knees, ignoring the stabbing pain. "Are you all right?"

Adan didn't speak. He simply looked at her and his eyes seemed to tell her that he was well, but as pissed off as she was.

"What's wrong?" She cut her glare to the two women who had followed her into the chamber. "Why can't he talk? Why can't he move?"

"Do not worry," Secka said as she reached down, taking Kara by the arm and pulling her to her feet. "It is only a temporary paralysis."

Kara tried to jerk away from Secka, but Daar rested her hand on the hilt of her sword and Kara stilled. Her heart pounded as her thoughts raced, wondering how she and Adan would escape this crazy mess. Who were these women? What did they want from her and Adan?

The crystal—for some reason they wanted her crystal. But why did they take Adan captive?

Unable to do anything but follow their instructions, Kara was forced against a wall. Her hands were manacled over her head by white fur-lined cuffs and a white linked chain that connected to a loop attached to the wall above her. A loop much like the one Adan was chained to. She struggled against the bonds, but she couldn't move.

"Echna comes." Secka backed away, as did Daar. They stood with their hands behind their backs, in a military stance.

Kara felt a blast of cold air over her naked body as it started to snow in the room. Only it was snowing in one spot. The flakes spun, and then Echna appeared, a glittering form at first, but then solid and whole.

She was holding Adan's sword.

The beautiful woman glanced to Adan, who stirred and pushed himself to a sitting position. His movements were slow, jerky, as if fighting off the drug. Kara felt relief that he could move, yet anger that he was tethered and unable to stand. She struggled again against her own bonds, her arms aching from being held over her head for so long. She'd never felt so vulnerable as she did being strapped to the cold wall with absolutely nothing on.

Not to mention the knives. She couldn't forget the knives.

Echna turned her gaze on Kara. Or actually to her breasts. Well, the pendant between her breasts. "Give me the crystal of your own free will," the woman said softly as her eyes met Kara's, "and I will release both you and your lover."

Free will. My own free will. That's why she hasn't taken it.

"No!" Adan yanked against his collar, fury searing his body and driving away the chill. "Do not give it to her." The ice-ghosts appeared on either side of him and held their blades to his neck. He ignored them. "They cannot take it from you, it must be given. Do not!"

"Damn you." Kara cut her furious glare from the women to Echna. "You touch him and you'll never get the crystal."

Echna held one hand up in a gesture obviously meant to stop Daar and Secka from taking any action against Adan. "You will both be my permanent guests until the crystal is turned over to me."

"Why do you want it so bad?" Kara tugged against her cuffs out of sheer frustration. "What's so important about this stupid pendant?"

The woman gave her a long and appraising look as she brushed a strand of snow-blonde hair over her shoulder. "Has he not told you?"

Kara frowned. "Told me what?"

"That you hold the key we have both been searching for." She glanced to Adan and then turned back to Kara. "With it he intends to destroy my people."

"That doesn't make sense." Kara shook her head. "It's just a pendant that my parents gave me before they abandoned me. He didn't know anything about it."

"So that is what you believe." Echna gave a soft laugh and ran her fingers along the edge of the blade of Adan's sword. "Clan Leader Valnez did not tell you that he has been searching for the crystal for himself."

The woman's face blurred as Kara's thoughts whirled and her cheeks burned. Her knees felt weak, and only her bonds forced her to keep standing.

Adan had only wanted the crystal? He had used her?

She fixed her gaze on him. "Is that true, Adan?"

The bastard sighed. "In a way—"

"I don't want to hear any more." It suddenly made sense—that's why he came to her. He was trying to find the crystal. That and a good fuck.

Well at least he *was* that—a good fuck. A great fuck, even. It wasn't like he meant anything more to her.

"Kara," Adan said sternly. "The witch only wants the crystal. Do not listen to her."

She swallowed and raised her chin, focusing on Echna and refusing to look at Adan. "What do you intend to do with it?" Kara asked.

"Protect my people." Echna clenched her fist and her jaw tightened. "The Clans wish to destroy our way of life."

"That is a lie." Adan growled and yanked at his chain. "It is this witch's desire to destroy the Clans."

Kara glared at them both. "Stop!"

A shadow passed over Echna's perfect features. In the next instant the woman seemed to grow, from a pale beauty to a dark witch looming above Kara, as if to eat her whole. Kara almost screamed with the terror that consumed her.

But then the darkness faded away, and Kara's heart began to beat again. Emotions flickered across Echna's features, as if she was battling herself.

The Ice-Witch gave a light shrug and examined Adan's sword. The symbols upon it were all but black beneath her touch, not gold like when Adan held it. "Very well," she said. "Perhaps you merely need time to think upon your circumstances." She turned to Secka and Daar, and handed Secka Adan's sword. "Guard them well and see that their every need is taken care of. And see to it that his sword is put away safely, in the vault."

When the Ice-Witch vanished in a swirl of snowflakes, Secka laid the sword against the far wall, in obvious defiance of Echna's orders. "Perhaps this will remind the man of his position. Of what he can and cannot have."

Daar moved closer to Kara who tried to draw away, but was too tightly bound. "Echna instructed that we see to their every need. I can think of many needs they surely have," the ice-ghost murmured.

Secka approached Kara, then looked from her to Adan with an obvious hunger in her pale eyes. "First, let us see to their supper."

Adan watched the fury in Kara's green gaze as she said, "I'm not hungry."

"You need your strength," he spoke in a low tone, his words intended to be an order.

Kara flung him a look that could easily have melted all the snow in Crystal Valley. "Fuck you."

The two ice-ghosts laughed as they exited through the wall-bubble, leaving Adan and Kara alone for the first time since coming to the ice palace. He glanced to his sword that mocked him from where it lay, and he clenched his fists and gritted his teeth.

His gaze returned to Kara and for a moment Adan could only look at his beautiful woman. With her arms bound above her head, her breasts jutted out, her nipples hard rosy peaks against her fair skin. Her trim waist led down to slender hips and his gaze rested on the soft blonde curls of her mound. He could scent her from across the room. If only he could taste her. If only they were in his home. He would take her to his bed and drive his cock into her, fucking her many times over.

"You used me." Kara's words held a hard, bitter edge to them.

He raised his eyes to meet her furious gaze. "I was searching for the crystal, truth. But I did not know you had it."

Her brows narrowed. "That first night, if you had found it in my home, you would have taken it."

Adan closed his eyes and pinched the bridge of his nose with his thumb and forefinger, trying to choose his words carefully. When he dropped his hand away and opened his eyes he sighed. There was nothing to tell her but the truth. "Aye."

A furious expression flashed across Kara's face. "And you would have left and never come back."

"Aye," he repeated quietly.

Her gaze was still angry, but he saw hurt there, too. "Bastard."

"But once I came to you the second night," Adan said, pulling against his chain as he tried to get closer to her, "I could not have stayed away for any reason. Even if I had found the crystal I would have done everything in my power to see you again."

Kara looked up at the skylight in the ceiling. "But you would have taken it. Without asking me."

When her gaze returned to him, Adan shook his head. "I do not know."

Her features changed and she adopted an indifferent attitude. "Whatever the case, it was fun fucking you while it lasted."

A low growl rumbled up from Adan's chest, and he could barely contain himself from telling her that it would never end. She was his, *forever*.

And then it occurred to him what the Cwen had said...the powercrystal had been hidden on Earth with another priceless treasure...and that he would need his heart and soul to find both.

Truth struck him as hard and cold as any ice wall.

Kara.

Kara was the priceless treasure of his heart.

"Why are we here?" Kara's voice cut into his realization and he turned his attention back to her. "Can you explain to me what in the hell is going on?"

"The crystal can be used as a weapon." Adan yanked at his chain as he spoke, his muscles bulging with the effort. "We must keep it from Echna."

"So that you can destroy her?"

"No." Adan released the chain and the links clattered against the cold floor. "We can only use it to change our destinies, not to make war with it."

"Oh, really." Skepticism laced her words and her chain rattled as she jerked against it. "You're a man. Men make war instead of solving their differences by compromise and treaty."

He scowled. "Kara—" he started just as a bubble bowed the wall outward.

Daar and Secka reappeared, carrying flagons along with trays of what appeared to be slabs of black bread, white cheese, chunks of meat, and pieces of a gray root. Warm smells filled the room, like a hot meal of roasted chicken, mashed potatoes and fresh baked bread.

Kara's stomach growled and her mouth watered.

Daar set one tray down and, with the point of her curved sword, pushed the tray and a flagon toward Adan, just close enough that he could reach the items but not her or the sword.

Secka brought the other tray up to Kara and smiled. Kara thought about refusing to eat, but it smelled so good. The bastard was right, she did need to keep her strength up.

"Are you going to let me down?" Kara pulled against her bonds. "I can't eat like this and my arms are going numb."

The woman plucked a chunk of bread from the tray and held it to Kara's lips. "Eat."

Ignoring Adan, Kara opened her mouth and took the piece of bread. Her eyes watered and her mouth puckered at the intensely sour and spicy taste. It was like eating a tequila lime tortilla chip with extra chili on it. The more she ate, though, the more she became used to the taste. The other items were just as weird—meat that tasted like peanuts, a spongy-cheesy substance that tasted like brie, and the gray root tasted of coffee. But all in all the meal was satisfying, if peculiar.

While she fed Kara, Secka would lightly brush Kara's nipples with the sleeve of her tunic, as if unintentional. Between the never-ending erotic heat of the pendant, and Secka's touches, Kara ached with need. Adan watched her eat as he devoured the food on his own tray. She ignored him as best as possible, but she couldn't help but want him, need him so badly she could just about scream.

"We were instructed to see to their every need." Daar said with a wicked smile when they finally finished eating and drinking from the flagons of bitter apple-flavored wine. "I know what they need now." And with a lingering look at Adan's naked body, she said to Secka, "Summon Eridon."

Chapter Seven

Daar said something else to Secka, who nodded and pressed the side of the box at her throat, and again spoke in the strange language that came from her lips instead of the box.

When Secka finished speaking, Daar's gaze traveled over Kara's body in a sensual perusal. "She is exquisite," the woman said. She licked her lips and glanced at Adan with a sly look. "I wonder how she tastes."

Adan growled as if in warning and his chain rattled.

Secka removed a white fur-lined scarf from around her throat. "Indeed," she said as she brought it close to Kara and gently brushed the fur over her nipples.

Kara gasped and tried to draw back, but with the way she was manacled there was nowhere to move. Despite herself, her pussy grew damp from the sensuous caress.

Daar glanced at Adan again, whose gaze held a mixture of heat and fury. His cock was rigid and thrusting up, proving his need for Kara and his arousal at the scene before him. Daar turned back and blew icy breath across Kara's skin. The chilly air traveled from her nipples all the way down to her pussy.

She nearly groaned. Her nipples tightened even harder and despite the fact that she was being held captive by these women, she was aroused. They hadn't even touched her with more than breath and the soft caress of fur.

At the same time the pendant grew warmer between her breasts, chasing the chill away with slow heat and yet again amplifying her sexual desires.

She startled as the wall beside her suddenly bowed. The crystal bubble appeared, and through it strode a gorgeous blond man. The bubble closed behind him, leaving again what appeared to be a solid wall. The man had hair, brows, and eyes as pale as the women, but he wore a crimson robe that stood out vividly against the white walls.

"My ladies," the man said through the box at his throat, giving a slight bow of his head and shoulders before straightening.

Daar moved to the man and pushed open his red robe, revealing a smooth, hairless, and powerful chest. His fair skin shone as though rubbed with oils, and Kara caught the light scent of musk.

"My lovely Eridon," Daar purred as she pushed the robe from his shoulders and down his arms. "You are such a good pet to come so quickly."

Kara's eyes widened as the fur-lined robe fell away, revealing his naked form. The only clothes Eridon wore were white bands around each of his biceps, and black fur-lined boots upon his large feet. Pale, wiry curls surrounded the base of his hardening erection.

Uh-oh. This couldn't be good. Kara swallowed. The women didn't intend to force her to have sex with this man, did they?

Eridon maintained his stance, but his cock continued rising to its full thickness. "What may I do for you, lady?"

Kara narrowed her eyes. Why was the man acting subservient to these women? He was obviously more powerful than them, yet he acted as if he were a slave, or a servant. By his expression, Eridon appeared to like being their pet. And it was obvious, too, that they cared for him. Not like an animal, but as a person they cherished.

"Come my darling concubine, let us show our guests the pleasures to be had in the ice palace." She glanced at Kara with a wicked look in her pale eyes. "Perhaps they would like to join us."

"Like hell," Kara yanked at her chains and fought against the nervousness filling her belly like bees captured in a jar. *They wouldn't... Oh, shit.*

"It is my duty and my pleasure to serve you in any way." Eridon gave another bow and then pulled each of his boots off and tossed them aside.

"I feel much too warm." Daar slipped out of her fur-lined cape and flung it on top of the boots. "Remove my clothing."

Slowly and sensually, Eridon took off each piece of Daar's clothing while Secka performed a striptease of her own. Secka's eyes moved from Adan to Kara. She unzipped her snowsuit to her mound, then opened it wide enough for her breasts to spill out. She grabbed her breasts and kneaded them before grasping her nipples and pulling at them until the pale pink buds turned darker, engorged with blood.

She smiled and kicked off her boots, then began stripping off her snowsuit. Her snow-blonde hair spilled over her shoulders and muscles worked at her tight belly as she pushed the suit down to her knees, revealing the white curls of her mound. She paused long enough to slip her fingers into her slit and then bring them to her mouth as she licked her juices away. Kara could even smell the crushed mint scent of the woman.

At the same time Secka performed her sensual striptease, Eridon opened the front of Daar's snowsuit, nibbling a path between her pale breasts and down to her navel. Kara relaxed a bit as she watched the trio's sexual play, feeling more confident that they didn't intend to involve her—other than torturing her, making her totally hot by performing in front of her and Adan.

The man opened Daar's suit all the way to the pale curls of her mound, and Kara bit her lip to quench her growing arousal. It didn't help.

After Eridon helped Daar out of her boots, he pushed her snowsuit from her arms, nibbling, licking, and sucking a path down her body. When her suit reached the floor, Eridon took her hand and helped the pale beauty step out of it.

Kara's desire for Adan grew as she remained riveted to the sexual play, and the sight of their perfect naked bodies. She tried to fight it, but she couldn't help the tingle in her pussy, the ache in her breasts, the tightening of her nipples.

She tore her gaze from the trio to meet Adan's eyes and the hunger there that she knew was for her. His cock was hard and rising up against his belly. No doubt he wanted her now as badly as she wanted him.

But damn it, he had *used* her to get to the crystal.

A moan of pleasure cut her attention back to Daar, whose silvery-white hair shielded her pale eyes while she bent forward, her hands in Eridon's pale hair. He was now on his knees, gripping her buttocks tightly as his mouth pressed against her pussy.

"Yes, pet." Daar's voice trembled. "More, give me more." The man groaned and pressed his face tighter to her folds.

The curls at both of Daar's and Secka's mounds were angel-hair white, and their folds a light shade of rose. Secka had moved beside the couple. Her tongue laved one of Daar's carnation pink nipples while her fingers pinched and pulled at the other one, and Daar moaned.

Kara almost moaned, too.

This is crazy. I'm out of my mind.

She twisted against her manacles, even though she knew it was useless. She wouldn't be able to escape even if she did manage to free herself. Hell, maybe she'd join them just to piss off Adan.

But she knew in her heart she wouldn't do that, no matter how big of a jerk he was.

All she could do was watch as Eridon licked Daar's pussy. "What a good pet you are." Daar gripped his hair tight in her hands. "My favorite, always my favorite."

"He is of the finest breeds in our well-stocked stable." Secka moved her mouth from Daar's nipple and slowly lowered herself to her knees. Her long pale hair brushed her nipples as she reached down to fondle Eridon's cock.

Kara squirmed, the need to come so powerful she could hardly stand it. From her side vision she saw that Adan had arranged himself so that he obscured the loophold from the trio's vision and Kara could see him tug at the chain with all his might, even as he watched the sexual display.

With a cry that echoed through the room, Daar climaxed. "Stop, Eridon," she cried. "No more." Her hips jerked against Eridon's face and he dug his fingers into the pale skin of her buttocks and buried his face impossibly harder against her pussy.

"Bad pet." Daar gripped his hair, pulled his head back and forced him to stop. "You are so very bad. I think you may deserve punishment."

A slight grin quirked the corner of his mouth, and Kara could tell Eridon had enjoyed himself. "Did I not please you, lady?"

Daar gave him a stern look. "You did not stop when I ordered you to."

He bowed his head, but a dimple remained in his cheek. "Yes, lady."

Daar waved to the floor. "On your back, pet."

Eridon obeyed, his muscles rippling as he settled himself on the floor, even though it was nearly as cold as the walls. He was a large man, easily as big as Adan. Kara wondered if their talk about concubines and stables of men—as well as his submissiveness—was just sexual play, or if he truly was a servant to these women. Whatever the case, he definitely looked like he was content to be a sex slave to Secka and Daar, if that's what he was.

Secka tossed a wicked glance to Kara, and then to Adan. "Are you certain you would not like to join us?"

Kara frowned and Adan's glare deepened.

Daar laughed and knelt beside Eridon who was flat on his back. She slowly stroked the man's cock with her small fingers while she watched Adan. "Are you certain, Clan Leader?"

Adan growled and jerked against the chains. He'd strangle every one of them if they touched Kara. At least they seemed content to play with themselves rather than touch his woman.

While the trio kept busy, Adan continually used his thoughtpower to call to the other Clan Leaders. He didn't know if Dane or Dominik would be able to hear him at such a distance, but he was certain the spybug would assimilate his call and transfer it to the Clans' headquarters. Eventually one of his knights would be alerted.

He gritted his teeth as Secka straddled Eridon's face and braced her hands to either side of his head. The concubine grasped her buttocks and began kneading her ass cheeks as he gave a low growl and sucked her clit.

Adan could picture doing the same with Kara, only in the privacy of his bedchamber. *When* they made it out of here alive, Adan intended to have Kara every way possible, multiple times.

Daar licked Eridon's erection, flicking her tongue along its length. He groaned against Secka's pussy when Daar slid her mouth over his cock and took him deep. She used her hand in tandem with her mouth as she traveled up and down his healthy length.

Daar stopped long enough to command him to wait for her permission to climax. Her only answer was Eridon's growl as he pleasured Secka. The woman was riding his face, now playing with her beautiful breasts, her head tilted back and her chest thrust forward.

Daar sucked him again, moving her hand faster up and down his cock. Eridon's body tensed and it was obvious he used supreme control to restrain himself from coming. Daar slipped Eridon's erection from her mouth, then straddled his hips in a graceful movement. With her eyes on Kara, she grasped the man's cock and placed it at the entrance of her pussy, before slowly sliding down the length of it.

Daar began riding Eridon, the muscles in her thighs flexing as she pushed herself up and down the length of his erection. "Remember pet," she said, sounding like she was almost out of breath, "as part of your punishment, you must not come until I am ready for you to."

Secka cried out and tipped forward, bracing her arms on the floor. Her pussy jerked against Eridon's face. Like he had with Daar, he only gripped her ass tighter, forcing one orgasm after another on her until she begged him to stop.

Daar continued fucking Eridon, the movements of her body growing faster and faster. Sweat glistened on her pale skin and her eyes rolled back in ecstasy. Whenever Daar rose up, Kara could see her slick juices on Eridon's thick cock.

Secka moved aside and settled herself on the floor as she watched the pair, braced one arm and began fingering her pussy with her free hand. Eridon grasped Daar by her hips. He thrust up, so hard that the sound of his flesh slapping hers was loud in the room.

"That's it, pet." Daar's breathing was harder yet and the palest pink tinged her pale cheeks. "Fuck me so perfect. Like the good breed you are."

Eridon pounded into Daar. Her breasts bounced with every thrust. He clenched his jaw and Kara had no doubt he was fighting his need to climax with all he had.

"Come," Daar commanded. "Come now, my Eridon!"

The man shouted and Daar screamed. Adan watched Kara as her body visibly shuddered. He was certain she almost came as she watched the two lovers climax together, and as Secka brought herself to another orgasm. Kara's gaze remained on the couple, watching the slowing of their thrusts until they stopped completely. The smells of their sex was thick in the air, mixing with that ever-present scent of peppermint.

Just when Adan thought the fuck-fest was over, Daar lay on her back. Secka settled over Daar, on her hands and knees, straddling Daar's face in a sixty-nine position.

Secka looked over her shoulder at Eridon. "Fuck my ass."

"My pleasure, lady." The man smiled as he moved behind Secka so that his knees were to either side of Daar's head, below Secka's pussy. Eridon rubbed his erection in Secka's folds until it glistened with her juices. He grabbed the woman's hips and then plunged his cock into the tight hole of her ass. Secka cried out, the sound one of obvious pleasure.

Adan's own cock ached at the thought of fucking Kara's ass. He could easily picture himself driving in and out of that rosy bud between her smooth, pale cheeks.

Secka and Daar, who were still in the sixty-nine position, began to lick each other's pussies while Eridon fucked Secka's ass. The sounds of moans and flesh slapping flesh filled the chamber.

Kara swallowed. She had never watched anyone fuck before, and the experience was definitely erotic. It was like she was living a bondage fantasy. Actually she *was* in the middle of a bondage fantasy, what with being chained to the wall. Only problem was, she didn't want to be there. Wherever "there" was. She wanted this all to end, to be back in her own home.

And to have Adan fucking the hell out of her.

No, no, no…he used me. She shook her head to clear out the images of Adan driving his cock in and out of her pussy so very hard, so very fast. Maybe even her ass. Kara couldn't help but think about the one and only time she and Adan had had sex, and how wild their passion had been.

Daar jerked against Secka's face, crying out as she came. Just moments later, Secka climaxed with a scream. Eridon pumped in and out of her ass several more times then gave a loud grunt as he reached orgasm.

No sooner had the trio stopped fucking one another than Secka was on her feet. She retrieved her sword from where it lay upon the heap of clothing, and moved to Adan's side.

With a wicked grin, she crouched beside him and held her blade to his throat. "I think I would like to fuck this one."

Heat flushed over Kara. Nothing doing. Adan was *hers*. No way was anyone going to touch her man. They'd be roadkill before she'd let anyone else fuck him.

"No!" she shouted, and Secka raised her eyebrows as she looked to Kara.

The pendant burned between Kara's breasts more intensely than it ever had before, glowing with her anger. She felt heat building in her body, hotter and hotter until she knew she would explode from it.

In the next moment fierce and intense heat filled the room, like a fireball had enveloped everything.

Coming from her!

The walls around them began to glow and moisture trickled down them.

Secka and Daar gasped while Eridon pulled Daar close to him as if to protect her from the sudden heat.

Their faces and bodies turned a brilliant shade of red, as if the heat was burning them.

More energy poured from the pendant, straight at the wall in front of Kara.

A crack and then a popping noise echoed through the room.

The wall began to melt.

First dripping in slow rivulets and then rushing down and across the floor. It poured over Kara's feet in a warm wave. Chunks of ice crashed down and then a portion of the wall wasn't there any more.

The heat abruptly stopped.

A hole the size of a truck had appeared in the wall and through it Kara could see an endless sea of snow. Freezing air blasted through the hole and Kara's entire body began to tremble. She stared in astonishment, unable to believe what had just happened in a matter of seconds. Everything had become more and more absurd and she could only stand there with her mouth open.

But Adan took advantage of everyone's shock. In a flash of movement, he disarmed Secka and shoved the heat-reddened woman away from him. She stumbled back and landed on her ass. He took her sword and slammed it against his chain, snapping the links like fragments of glass, leaving only the collar around his neck.

With the roar of a fierce predator, he rounded on the three who were naked and weaponless.

"On your knees." His words were as cold as the bitter air coming through the hole in the wall.

When he raised the sword, the two women complied. Daar and Secka both held their heads high like proud warriors. Eridon clenched his jaw and looked ready to go for Adan's throat, but Secka said in a commanding tone, "Kneel, you fool."

Kara pushed aside her bewilderment, ignored the bitter wind pouring in through the hole, and struggled against her bonds. She did her best to try and slip out of the fur-lined cuffs, but they were far too snug. Wind from outside blasted into the room and Kara knew that normally she wouldn't last much longer without clothing. The pendant grew warmer between her breasts and heat rushed through her body, just enough to keep her from freezing to death.

Adan was so furious he was ready to storm the palace and find that Ice-Witch bitch. But he had to get Kara out of there and safely to Crystal Valley. If that was even possible.

He slowly backed from the trio and bent down to scoop up his own sword from where it lay beside the pile of clothing. Immediately the runes sparked with fire. Holding a weapon in each hand, he moved closer to Kara, and with one quick slice of his sword, he hacked her chains and she dropped. "Shit," she muttered as she landed on her already battered knees and more pain shot through her.

"Dress in their clothing," Adan ordered.

Kara ached from the fall, but scrambled to her feet. Without hesitation she pulled on a fur-lined pair of pants and one of the shirts, followed by gloves and boots which were both too big for her, but would do. The women were taller than Kara, and the pants bunched up on her boots and the shirt fell to her thighs. She was still shivering, but the clothing was quickly warming her body.

The whole time Adan held up both swords, prepared to handle whoever might try to stop them.

When she was completely dressed, she grabbed Eridon's fur-lined robe and boots, and prayed they would be enough to protect Adan out in the snow when they made their escape.

"Hold this." Adan handed her one of the ice-ghost's swords and she almost dropped it from its weight. She managed to raise it while she glared at the trio. How did the women carry, much less battle with such heavy weapons?

In just a matter of seconds, Adan had stepped into the boots and wrapped the robe tightly around his body. Somehow it managed to stay snug around him, as if made to keep out the cold and snow.

When they were both dressed, Adan took the sword from her and pointed to the remaining clothing. "Take the scarves and bind their hands."

"They'll freeze to death." Kara hesitated. "We can't just leave them here, naked."

Adan kept his eyes on the three. "The bonds will only hold them long enough to give us a head start. They will free themselves easily enough."

Kara breathed a sigh of relief and did as Adan instructed. She didn't want to be responsible for anyone's deaths, even if they had kidnapped her.

The front of their bodies was still a bright red, in contrast with their backsides, which was their normal pale coloring. Somehow the power of the pendant had burned them, and Kara didn't like knowing she was responsible for it.

In moments she had bound the women's hands with the two long scarves, and then Eridon's wrists with the extra pair of pants. Amazingly their skin didn't feel nearly as cold as Kara felt, even with the clothes she now wore.

She tied the knots as tight as she could then hurried to Adan's side. He offered her a look that gave her a certain amount of confidence despite their bleak situation.

"Run," he ordered her. "Run with everything you have."

Chapter Eight

Without hesitation, Kara bolted through the gaping hole in the ice-wall, jumping over the small mound of ice that had formed at the bottom of the opening, and into the freezing air. Her booted feet immediately sank into a huge drift and she pitched forward, face-first into the freezing snow.

A large hand grabbed her by the scruff of her neck. Kara came up, sputtering snow and blinking frost out of her eyes. Her eyes stung and her cheeks burned, and more of the white stuff packed her nostrils.

"Move!" Adan didn't give her a chance to breathe. He released her jacket, grabbed her hand, and practically dragged her with him. Somehow he plowed ahead like a bulldozer, as if walking across flat ground rather than through three feet of powdery snow.

With her free hand she wiped the snow from her nose while she did her best to keep up. "How are we going to escape them?" she asked, her words and her breath coming out as a white cloud in the chill air.

"Pray," Adan rumbled, his face a mask of fury and determination. He held his sword in one hand like an avenging angel. His red cape scraped the snow behind him and she was sure he must be freezing. But he forged ahead, not complaining, a fierce look in his dark eyes.

Kara's hands and cheeks grew icy while they stumbled through the drifts, and her fingers and toes numbed despite the gloves and boots. Fortunately, the pendant chased away a lot of the chill. She could barely see through the frost on her eyelashes. She tried to rub it away with her sleeve, but that only made it worse as she coated more snow across her face in the process.

"Let me give you my pendant." Kara tried to reach the crystal tucked away beneath her tunic. "It'll warm you. You're only wearing a cape. You need it more than I do."

Adan shook his head. "I will last long enough."

Her gaze shot to his. "Long enough for what?"

He gave her a scowl and then looked toward the horizon. "Woman, you ask too many questions."

Kara concentrated on trying to make it through the snow instead of talking. The logical part of her brain told her she needed to conserve her strength. A coppery taste like blood filled her mouth from the exertion, and her side ached. She tripped again, but Adan kept her from falling, his grip firm on her hand.

She looked over her shoulder and saw that to the other side of the palace was a grove of snow-covered trees, and she wished they were headed in that direction. At least then they would have someplace to hide. Out here there was nothing but white.

Kara stumbled forward yet again, and Adan dragged her back up. Before them only miles and miles of snow blanketed the landscape. In the distance a glittering snow-capped mountain range crouched on the horizon, taunting them. It didn't take much to realize it was too far to reach in time. She shivered more with every step they took and her teeth chattered so loud it was possible the ice-ghosts could hear the noise from the palace.

A large black spot caught her attention. It shot toward them from the direction of the mountains. The form drew closer and closer at amazing speed, but she couldn't tell what it was. She was about to ask Adan when she heard shouts and then a sound like a very large bee, coming from behind.

Kara's heart pounded so hard her chest ached. She cast a look over her shoulder and her gut clenched at the sight of a large snowmobile, in the shape of a giant white jelly bean. It raced across the snow—or rather, *above* the snow.

She whipped her attention back to the snowy landscape ahead. Her breathing grew more ragged. Her body ached from the cold, and her battered knees screamed with pain. But she knew Adan must be faring much worse than her, clad only in the cape and boots, and without the pendant to help alleviate the chill.

The hum of the vehicle was at their backs, and Kara's stomach pitched. She knew it was hopeless. They would never escape.

Adan's concern for Kara and the *L'sen* Crystal mounted. He pressed forward, his eyes focused on the black windcraft in the distance. He mind-spoke with Dominik. *Hurry!*

The cape took some of the chill away, but snow had slowly crusted Adan's body beneath it and he was certain his balls would fall off. The slicing cold would have been enough to drive any man to his knees, but Adan's only thought was to save Kara and that gave him the strength to drive forward. Somehow warmth radiated from her straight to him, and he knew the crystal surely had something to do with it. There was no other explanation.

The ice-ghosts' snowflyer neared from behind, but the Clans' much faster windcraft bore down on them up ahead.

"What's that?" Kara shouted and pointed before she stumbled again.

His mouth set in grim determination, Adan jerked her up. "Salvation."

Even as Dominik guided the windcraft toward them, the buzzing sound of the snowflyer eased as it neared. The ice-ghosts were preparing to snatch up Adan and Kara before the windcraft could reach them.

The Clans' craft crested a snowdrift, a large octagonal-shaped ship. Adan didn't stop to look back as he pulled Kara closer to the windcraft.

Hair at Adan's nape prickled in warning.

He dropped and pushed Kara down into the snow just as a beam of white light shot over their heads and slammed into the windcraft.

"Keep going," Adan ordered as Kara emerged from the snow, sputtering and taking deep gulps of chill air. "Crawl."

A second and third streak of white shot over their heads as they pressed forward on their hands and knees. The bolts missed the windcraft as the lithe black ship veered out of its way. Dominik returned fire, arrows of green light snapping and crackling through the air, one after another.

Adan threw a look over his shoulder in time to see the lasers punch holes through the lesser craft's outer walls. The screeching sound of torn metal rent the air. The acrid smell of burning electronics filled his nostrils and singed his throat. Through the clear face-shield, he saw fear in the pale eyes of the ice-ghosts piloting the craft, and he felt a moment's regret.

The snowflyer exploded.

Green fire boiled in the air. Shrapnel soared over their heads and drove into the snow.

Adan threw himself over Kara, pushing her deep within a huge drift. Heat rushed over his body and the cape burned against his skin. Pain stabbed his backside like a thousand knives and then darkness slammed his mind shut.

Kara couldn't breathe. Adan's body crushed hers into the snowbank. She was pinned too tightly to move.

Somewhere in the distance she heard voices, but she was suffocating. Stars sparked in her head and her lungs burned. Gradually her body began to warm and go numb. The cozy warmth made her feel like snuggling into a ball.

Sleep. Yes, sleep.

Just as she began to slip toward a black abyss, Adan's weight was suddenly lifted from her back. A pair of hands grabbed her under the arms, yanked her out of the drift, and laid her carefully on the snow-covered ground.

"The woman is turning blue," a man's voice said, and dimly she saw his face hovering above her. The man fastened his mouth to hers and warm breath entered her lungs. When he raised his head, Kara coughed and sucked in a lungful of the acrid air, immediately coughing again. Her body seized from the cold and she struggled to breathe despite all the smoke billowing around them. She began trembling uncontrollably as the illusion of warmth fled her, replaced by biting pain in every one of her fingers and toes.

Through muted hearing, the sound of voices grew farther away. She thought she heard "get Valnez to Ana and fast."

Her eyelids fluttered, the crystallized snow flaking into her eyes as she tried to remember what had just happened.

"Whoever the hell you are, you're certainly not an ice-ghost," the man muttered as he scooped her into his arms and started carrying her as she coughed against his chest. He strode toward the large black thing that had flown over the snow, straight toward her and Adan.

A spaceship. It must be a spaceship, her hazy mind told her.

Her fog-filled brain vaguely took in the wreckage surrounding them. Smoke curled in the air and steam hissed. Blood spattered the snow and scraps of metal were scattered as far as she could see.

Even as she continued to cough from the smoke, she moved her gaze to the man carrying her. His long blond hair swung past his shoulders and his gray eyes were as cold as the surrounding snow. He had an angry set to his jaw and his brows were a fierce line above his hooded eyes.

Panic seized her as she began slowly coming back to awareness—she hadn't seen Adan since he shoved her into the snow.

"Adan," she tried to say, but it came out in an unintelligible croak.

The man treated her to a scowl, but then his features softened. "Valnez has a hell of a lot of explaining to do."

She shook her head and tried again. "Where — where's Adan?" The words came out as a scratchy whisper, but at least she didn't sound like a frog.

Instead of answering her, the man stepped beneath the black ship that hovered above the ground. "Now," he growled.

Orange light rose up from the ground and encased them. Kara felt a strange vibration throughout every part of her body, and then a tingling sensation, like a million spiders crawling over her skin.

They were outside in the snow, and then they weren't, as fast as that.

Kara's head spun and she thought she was going to puke. When she could focus, and her stomach wasn't about to heave its contents, she saw she was in a cramped room. A woman bent over a figure on a table nearby. Strange electrical equipment and three long table-like beds took up most of the room.

Kara's throat worked when saw that Adan was on one of them. Face down, his cape melted against his skin and metal sticking out from his backside.

"Adan!" Kara fought to get away from the blond man's hold, but he wouldn't release her. "Damn it, let me go!" she shrieked. Tears stung her eyes when she saw that Adan wasn't moving, and terror gripped her heart.

"Take us out of here, Dominik," the man holding her said as Kara fought to get away from him.

"We'll be home in no time." A disembodied voice responded. "Hold tight."

The ship lurched forward, but the man holding Kara didn't even stumble. "Where do you want the woman, Ana?"

"Set her on that table." The uniformed woman pointed to the bed beside Adan. "And then you can give me a hand, Dane."

"You're not just going to set me aside!" Kara started beating on the man called Dane, tears streaming down her face. "You bastard! Let me *down*!"

With a sigh of irritation, he let her slowly slide to her feet. "You are going to regret this."

The moment Kara's feet touched the floor, her knees gave out and her entire body went limp. She started to drop but the man caught her beneath her arms.

"Adan will live." Dane swept her up and deposited her on one of the other beds where she collapsed like a rag doll. "He is going to have a hell of a sore ass, but he will live."

"He *is* a tough bastard." Ana gave Kara a grim look as she brought a pair of large forceps out from a cabinet. She proceeded to remove the chunk of metal that had pierced the cape and was buried in Adan's muscular ass. Blood flowed over the cape and onto the table.

Kara's stomach churned. She leaned over the side of the bed and hurled all over Dane's boots.

Chapter Nine

Adan slid his legs over the side of the bed as he pushed himself to a sitting position. He clenched his teeth as the incredible pain in his ass burned like fire. His feet hit the med-wing floor with a thump as he hurried to relieve the pressure. His legs nearly gave out on him and he had to grip the bed's mattress to keep from falling. Cool air brushed his naked skin and the wounds at his back burned from the slight contact.

Despite the pain, Adan could only think of finding Kara, ensuring she was safe and well. Why hadn't she come to see him in the medical wing? He intended to find out.

Ana, the Clans' Chief Medical Officer, strode into the med-room. The commanding brunette wore the knight's jumpsuit, which sported a med patch just below the Blackstar sword and star insignia.

"What in the stars' names do you think you are doing?" She glared when she spotted Adan on his feet. "I instructed you to remain in bed until I gave you official clearance."

He gritted his teeth against the pain. "I am ready to be released now."

Ana stared at him for one long moment, as if sizing up his determination. "Stubborn bastard." She reached into the cabinet and brought out a hypo. In moments she had filled the clear syringe with a yellow liquid and approached Adan with it. "Turn around, brace your hands on the bed."

His frown deepened as he glanced at the hypo. "I do not need anything."

She met his gaze head on, never flinching. "You do and you *will*."

It was Adan's turn to glare, but he knew better than to argue with Ana when she was in her domain. Here she was in command and his knights would follow *her* instructions, even if it meant pinning him to the floor so that she could administer the hypo or any other form of medical torture she wished to inflict upon him.

Grudgingly, Adan turned and braced his hands on the bed. He nearly shouted when she applied the hypo to his sore ass and fire rushed his body like a solar flare.

"There." The Chief Medical Officer backed up as he turned around. She had a satisfied expression on her face, as if pleased to have caused him some measure of pain since he was ignoring her directions. "That ought to relieve some of the soreness, but you are certainly going to wish you had listened to me."

"Not likely." As long as he was with Kara, he would be more than all right.

Ana "humphed" and strode across the room where she retrieved his pants and boots and dropped them onto the med-bed. "You may want to leave the shirt off, at least for today, because it is going to hurt like the devil to wear clothing," she tossed over her shoulder as she turned and walked out of the room.

Adan did not intend to have his clothing on for long. Not once he found Kara.

Just as he finished pulling on his breeches and boots, Dane strode into the med-room. The knight wore a fierce expression on his carved features. "You should be in bed. We cannot afford for you to not be at your optimal performance."

With a scowl Adan flexed his muscles and ignored the pain the movement caused in his back. His ass burned like hell where the breeches fit snugly, but the pain was lessening from the hypo Ana had administered.

"As I have told you before," Adan replied, forcing himself to rein in his anger, "You would do well to mind your own concerns and not mine."

The blond man looked like a furious Viking of long, long ago. "Your ability to lead the Clans *is* my concern."

Adan gave Dane a glare that would have flattened a lesser man. "If you have nothing further to say, you'd best get out of my way."

For a moment the knight studied Adan. "You endangered the mission, endangered our very world by your dalliance with the Earth woman."

Clenching his fists, Adan said, "That is also none of your concern."

"It is, friend." Dane stepped close enough that Adan caught the scent of the knight's anger, saw it flash in his gray eyes. "You fucked her. You did not simply take the crystal and be done with it, you fucked her."

It was all Adan could do to hold back from punching his fellow Clan Leader. "You tread on dangerous ground, *friend.*"

But Dane was not finished. "You endangered not only your life, but all of our lives by not taking the crystal to begin with, and by being captured by that ice-bitch. We nearly lost a good craft, not to mention you. And all over a good fuck."

This time Adan did not hold back. He slammed his fist into Dane's jaw. The man came back with a punch that landed on Adan's cheekbone, and stars burst behind his eyes. Just as he hauled back to hit Dane again, two knights took hold of each of Dane's arms and dragged him back.

Dominik appeared between them, a fierce look in his green eyes. "Dane may not have approached the situation in the most diplomatic manner. However, as we are your fellow Clan Leaders, you do owe us an explanation for your actions."

Of all of them, Dominik was the most level-headed, the one to restrain his emotions and to choose words instead of fists to solve a fight. But at the moment he looked ready to lay into Adan like Dane had.

The knights released Dane, who folded his arms and stood behind Dominik. He stepped forward, still glaring at Adan. "Answer," Dane demanded.

Adan looked from one Clan Leader to the other, and some of his anger lessened. In their place, he would be looking for answers as well. He considered telling them that he believed Kara to be the treasure to be sought along with the crystal. But he decided to wait until he consulted with the Cwen.

"I make no excuses for my actions," he finally said. "What Kara and I shared—that is not up for discussion. But I will tell you that I did not know she had the crystal until it was too late. Echna's ice-ghosts had Kara before I could get to her. I had no choice but to allow myself to be taken as well. Otherwise I would not have retrieved the crystal and her life would have been lost."

Both men remained silent as if absorbing Adan's words. "Very well," Dominik said after a moment. "What is done is done. Now we must take the crystal from the woman and implement the plan."

"You will not take anything from her." Adan's words were sharp and his anger rose again. "When the time is right I will discuss it with her and we will proceed from there."

Dominik gave a reluctant nod of acceptance, and Dane scowled and turned on his heel.

Kara paced the length of her room — the room she'd been confined to for her stay on this snowbound planet. For two days she'd been cooped up, a prisoner, and not allowed to see Adan.

It was really pissing her off.

At least it was Adan's chambers that she was stuck in. She could tell by his masculine scent that lingered in the air, not to mention his clothing stored in closets and chests. She had explored every inch of the room in her boredom, had studied Adan's holo-vids as Lilli called them. Lilli was the one person Kara had been able to talk to whenever the woman brought meals to her. She was a beautiful and kind woman, but Kara had the feeling that she knew Adan better than Kara would have liked. Not that it mattered what he had done before he met her.

Hell, why should it matter at all? she thought as she continued to pace the room.

The holo-vids were few, but in those he kept, Kara had seen a pretty brunette with a dimple in one cheek, a dark-haired boy with a matching dimple, and Adan standing proudly with them. Her heart ached for him when Lilli told her that his wife and child had died in a battle at the end of the Age of Sorcery. Here was a man who had lost two people he had loved, his family. It seemed far worse than Kara never having had a family to lose.

Kara remembered a quote by Tennyson: "'Tis better to have loved and lost than never to have loved at all." She wasn't so sure that was true, but she had never known it for herself.

Yesterday she had been visited by the hulking man, Dane, who had questioned her about who she was, what she had been doing at the ice palace, how Adan got there, and how she came by the crystal. She had thought about refusing to answer, but the man was so large and his scowl so intimidating that she had grudgingly given him the answers, the best she could. By the time Dane asked her how she knew Adan, she'd been so angry that she said she'd fucked him once or twice and to leave her the hell alone.

And that's exactly what Dane had done. She hadn't seen the bastard since, and the door had been kept locked so that she couldn't leave this stupid room.

Adan's room was all right for a room, not much different from what you'd find on Earth, only in more space age-y pewter-colored materials. A nice sized bed crouched in the center, and various pieces of furniture were scattered around. It was such a contrast from the ice palace. Here, instead of sterile white, the walls were in warm shades of taupe. Murals of a countryside in the springtime flowed from one wall to the next. With all the snow outside, she imagined the planet's residents must surely get spring fever big time.

Yet what she'd seen of the landscape from the bedroom window was stunning. She especially liked the Mirror Mountains and the way they reflected the valley upon their glittering surfaces.

She wasn't sure she could get used to the spaceships flying around, though, or all these futuristic knights. Not that she'd have to. As soon as Adan was up and about, she intended to make him take her back home. She didn't belong here.

Kara paused in the middle of the room and ran her finger along the crystal star sculpture perched on the table. Her knees still ached from the battering they had taken at that Ice-Witch's palace, but not too badly. Her pendant seemed to heal her faster than normal. At least that's what it felt like when the heat from it surged through her body. The problem was that it still made her horny as hell, and nothing she did relieved the ache like Adan could.

Their kidnapping by the ice-ghosts — that all seemed like a dream now. She could hardly believe she'd been held prisoner, had watched three people have sex, melted a hole in the wall, fought her way through the snow with Adan, and then had been rescued. But not before he had been seriously injured.

At least Dane had told her Adan would be all right.

She brought her hand to the crystal that lay between her breasts and fingered it. "What's so important about it?" she murmured aloud. "Is it really magic?"

How had that wall melted like it did? If only she could melt the wall before her and escape out into the snow, rather than stay here inside. She had always loved the snow, but she wasn't sure she'd always want to live in it. Kind of like living in Antarctica or something.

The pendant continually sent a warm tingling sensation throughout her body and caused her to be in a constant state of arousal. Her breasts ached for Adan's touch, her nipples were taut, dying for his hot mouth, and her pussy was so wet, needing his cock deep inside her. It was driving her nuts.

The sarong she was wearing didn't help. It was fastened to one shoulder with a gold clasp. Her other shoulder was bare, as was the side of one breast, the curve of her waist and one hip. The filmy emerald green material clung to her curves, caressing her skin with every movement she made, like Adan's fingertips skimming across her body. It whirled around her ankles and bare feet in a whisper-soft movement.

She rubbed her wrists where the cuffs had been before Dane removed them with some kind of device. No matter how she tried not to think about him, no matter how she tried to remain pissed off at him, Kara couldn't get Adan off her mind. Once she had known he was fine, she couldn't help but feel betrayed by the fact that he'd been after her crystal all along. "You owe me some answers, Adan," she said aloud. "And I'm running out of patience."

Kara let her hand fall away from the pendant and she moved to the shielded picture window. She touched the pane and the shield shimmered and faded away, letting in the gray light of the day. Outside she saw the Tower of Light that Lilli had pointed out, which looked an awful lot like a giant penis, kind of like a larger version of her crystal pendant. She had to laugh. What a strange thing to have sitting beside a frozen lake.

Kids played in the snow around the pillar, having snowball battles, and creating elaborately formed miniature cities of snow and ice creatures. Considering the

Clans had been on this planet for a decade, it was no wonder they were so good at ice and snow art. She had wondered why people didn't ice-skate on the lake, but according to Lilli an underground hot springs caused the ice to be weak in some places, and they didn't want to chance anyone falling through.

Spacecraft zoomed around and people trudged through the snow, going about their daily duties. Lilli had told Kara much about the colony and how the people came to be on this planet. She had explained what the people were doing as they worked in the snow, and how they survived on what the planet had to offer. There was even a colony of people indigenous to the planet who lived below the ground and fed on fish and plants that grew only in the caverns, and captured unwary snowrabbits that ventured into the caves. Apparently they'd been asked if they would like to come to the surface to join the Clans, but had refused.

She placed her hand to the now unshielded pane and it felt cool to the touch. With a sigh she rested her forehead against the glass and her breath fogged it, obscuring her vision. The memory of the first time she'd seen Adan, when she was looking through her own window, came rushing over her. It seemed so long ago, yet it had been what, mere days? A week, maybe more? She couldn't remember anymore. It seemed like a lifetime that she'd known him.

Just as she leaned back to wipe the fog from the window, a pair of large hands clasped her waist from behind.

Kara yelped and tried to turn, but a man pressed his length to hers. He buried his face in the crook of her neck, his stubbled cheek abrading the soft skin. Instantly she knew it was Adan, from his unique scent and the feel of his muscled body molded against hers. Her pendant sent more fire through her, stimulating her beyond belief. Oh, God how she needed him to fuck her, and now.

"I have missed you, love," came his low, seductive voice in her ear. He slowly trailed his fingers down the side of her body that was bare, from the curve of her breast to her hip and back. His calloused fingertips were rough against her soft skin.

"Adan." She shivered and her nipples tightened against the gauzy fabric of her sarong. Her pussy grew even wetter and her body ached for Adan more than ever. "I've missed you, too."

Slowly he turned her so that she was looking up at him. His chest was bare and she saw that healing wounds scaled his arms, and he had a brutal-looking gash above one eye. It looked like someone had just punched him from the way it was red and starting to darken. She noticed the ice-ghosts' collar had been removed from his neck, but that his skin had been rubbed raw from the leather.

"Why didn't you come to see me?" he murmured as he touched one finger to her chin.

"Dane wouldn't let me out of this room," Kara replied as she melted at the sight of his injuries. She wanted to caress him, to care for him. To have wild, crazy sex with him. But at the same time she was still angry. "I really should kick your ass, you know," she said with her best attempt at a scowl.

Adan winced. "Would you mind waiting until my ass has healed?"

The corner of Kara's mouth quirked and she did her best not to laugh. "Maybe." But then her features went serious again. "What's so important about this crystal?"

He sighed and rubbed his stubble in a movement that made her feel like he was stalling for time. "I am not sure I am the right one to tell you."

"If not you, then who?" She tried to pull away, but he wouldn't release the hold he had on her.

Again he took a moment to answer. "An advisor to our people," he finally replied. "She will explain the value of the crystal to you. What it means to our world."

Frustration welled up inside her. "Dammit, I want *you* to tell me."

"I promise that all your questions will be answered." He tweaked the curl over her forehead. "And if you are not satisfied, you can kick my ass then."

This time she couldn't help a small grin. But then her smile turned back into a frown. "You used me, Adan. I don't like being used."

His lips set in a grim line before he said, "I am sorry, Kara. I do not know how to make it up to you."

"I do." Kara placed her hands on his shoulders, taking care not to touch his wounds. She rose up on her toes and whispered in his ear, "Fuck me."

Chapter Ten

Adan's gut clenched as Kara's soft voice whispered her lustful command. He slid his hands from her shoulders to her elbows and back as he studied her features. Her eyes were dark green and her lips moist and slightly parted. The sarong she wore revealed the curve of one breast all the way down to her hip and his cock ached to take her *now*.

"Well, come on." She reached for the fastenings of his breeches. "I'm tired of waiting."

Adan caught her hands and held them within his own. "Do you think that sex will make everything right between us?"

Cocking her head to one side, Kara looked up at him. "No…but it'll be fun."

Adan frowned. "I do not want you to think that I merely wish to fuck you. I want more, Kara."

"More what?" She furrowed her brows. "You can't be thinking about a relationship. I mean you live here, in the future, on an ice-planet. I live in the past on Earth. I have a life there, my friends, and my job."

Adan brought one hand up to cup her cheek. He caressed the soft skin with his thumb, moving it to the moist corner of her mouth and back. "Give it time, love. Give *us* time. That is all I ask."

Lost in the power of his words, Kara closed her eyes as he continued to stroke her cheek. Something deep within called to her, more than simply the desire to have sex with Adan. She felt a connection with him that she had never experienced before, with any man.

Was it worth exploring, even for a little while?

No. This is crazy. Go home while you have the chance!

The thought of going home suddenly made her stomach hurt. It felt wrong, somehow. Like that choice would ruin everything, from the past to the present and the future, too.

With a shuddering sigh she opened her eyes. "All right," she whispered as her gaze met his dark eyes. "I don't promise anything, but I'll give you—us—some time to figure this all out." The thought of leaving him tore at her again, but still she added, "If and when I decide to go home, you have to let me. That's the deal."

For a long moment Adan just looked at the beauty before him. He couldn't bear the thought of her leaving him, but he did not want to force her if she chose not to stay...

Instead of answering, he lowered his head and sought out her lips with his. She opened for him willingly, allowing his tongue to slip into her mouth. He slid his fingers from her cheek into her curls, and cupped the back of her head. With his other hand he drew her body tight to his and pressed his erection against her belly.

Her warmth heated him, the taste of her filled him, and her scent of spring and woman surrounded him. No, he could never get enough of this woman and he *would not* let her go. He would win her heart, no matter the cost.

Kara's kiss became more urgent and her soft moans fired his loins. He deliberately kept the pace slow, wanting to make love to her, not just fuck this woman who had captured his heart in such a short span of time.

When she placed her palms against his chest, he was sure she could feel the thundering of his heart. She moved her hands to his shoulders and he flinched when her fingers gripped his wounds.

She tore away from his kiss, her cheeks flushed and her lips swollen. An apologetic look crossed her sweet face. "I'm sorry. I forgot."

With a smile he captured both her hands in his and brought her knuckles to his lips. "You could never really hurt my flesh, love. Only my heart."

Kara bit her lip at the feel of the sensual caress of his mouth kissing each of her knuckles in turn. She wanted him with a need so fierce that she would have scaled his body and wrapped her legs around his waist if he hadn't been injured. Instead she let him set the pace, all the while dying to feel his naked body against hers, his cock deep within her core.

With a rumble of desire, Adan scooped her into his arms, pressing her against his broad chest, and she laughed in surprise. She wrapped her arms around his neck, but this time she took care not to grab the wounds on his shoulders. He carried her toward the bed and gently set her down beside it, until her bare feet reached the cool floor.

For a long moment he simply stroked his fingers through her curls and looked at her. The curls sprang back with every stroke and he smiled. Electricity zinged through her belly and straight to her pussy. God, he was so handsome. The fierce spark in his eyes, the straight line of his jaw, his stubbled cheeks and his hard packed body. Everything about him set her on fire.

"You do know you're about to make me lose my mind, don't you?" She reached up and caught his hand in hers, then brought it slowly down to her breast. "Touch me, Adan. Feel me."

"Aye, love." Adan brought his other hand up and began kneading both of her breasts through the gauzy fabric of her sarong. "I feel you beneath my fingertips, and I feel you in my heart and soul."

Kara braced her hands on his chest, his muscles rippling beneath her fingertips. It amazed her how much she was enjoying this slow torment. For the first time in her sexual life she was truly *experiencing* how it felt to be made love to. And she had to admit, it was incredible.

He slid one hand up to the clasp of her sarong and released it. Instantly, the filmy material fluttered over her fair skin, caressing her breasts, her waist, her hips as it fell to the floor, leaving her completely naked. Gripping her shoulders, he brought his mouth to hers while he slowly rubbed his hands up and down her arms.

She moaned, holding back a stronger cry that struggled to break free. His tongue darted between her lips, and her thoughts whirled. She became dizzy with the strength of her need, and she wasn't sure any more which way was up and which way was down, or even where she was at that moment in time.

When Adan raised his head again, Kara was finding it hard to breathe. She'd heard about lovemaking like this, read about it in romance novels, but had never experienced anything so sensual in all her life. She couldn't believe this fierce man could be so gentle, so loving, and it tugged at her heart.

Kara brought her hands to the fastenings of his pants, wanting, needing to touch him. Before he could say anything, she put a finger to his lips and murmured, "Shhhh. It's my turn."

Adan grunted, He did not want to turn over control to Kara, but the moment she reached for his breeches and brushed her hand across his cock, he could no longer think past wanting her hands and mouth upon him.

With agonizing slowness, Kara pulled apart the closure on his breeches and slipped the material down over his hips. His cock thrust out at her, begging for her attention.

Settling herself on her knees in a graceful movement, Kara traced the fat vein along the bottom of his erection with her fingertip.

"You have the biggest cock I've ever seen," she murmured.

Fierce jealousy slammed into Adan that she had been with other men. He certainly intended to be the *last* man she would ever be with.

Kara circled the head of his cock with her finger and Adan sucked in his breath. "If you do not stop your teasing, witch, I shall not be held accountable for what I am going to do to you."

Looking up at him, she gave a sexy grin that did nothing to alleviate the strength of his need for her.

"I thought you wanted it slow, big guy."

Adan nearly groaned aloud. Instead he tipped his head back, closed his eyes, and simply let himself feel what Kara was doing to him.

Her warm breath blew over the head of his cock and this time he did groan. She gave a soft laugh and cupped his balls with one hand while she stroked his staff with her other.

Then he felt her tongue flick across the head of his cock and he clenched his buttocks, wincing from the pain of his wounds that quickly eased into pleasure. In spite of the Clans' doctors and technology, and the hypo, his rapidly healing injuries still ached. But the ache became nothing but a slow burn that melded into the heat of his body, the fire of his desire for Kara.

"Sorcerers be damned." He opened his eyes and looked down to see her green eyes staring right back at him. "I believe I may be forced to tie you to my bed and take you now."

She raised her eyebrows—looking intrigued at the idea—and his cock jumped in her hand. "Maybe." With a mischievous smile she slipped her lips over his erection and took him deep in her mouth, to the back of her throat.

"Aye, that's it, love." He reached for her head and gripped his hands in her curls as she slowly moved up and down his staff. His own insistence on taking it slow was coming back to haunt him. He wanted her to hurry, wanted her to suck harder and longer and he wanted to come in her beautiful mouth.

Adan watched his staff move in and out of her lips. He loved the picture she made, down on her knees while she was looking up at him. Her green eyes always grew so dark when she was aroused, like the forests he had lived near before the Age of Sorcery.

Kara took her time sucking his cock, alternately licking him from balls to tip and sucking on him with a force that almost brought him to his knees with the need to come. She teased him unmercifully, never letting him get close enough, always backing off before he reached climax.

When he could take no more, Adan let out a low growl, forced Kara to release his cock, grabbed her by her shoulders, and brought her up to face him. He hooked his index finger under her chin and raised her head. "I should turn you over my knee and spank you."

Kara shivered at the mere idea and licked her lips. "Before or after you tie me up?"

Adan let out another growl, only this time much louder and fiercer. He grabbed her slim waist with his large hands, caught her up and laid her down on the bed so fast she didn't have time to catch her breath.

She watched him as he kicked off his boots and finished removing his pants in slow deliberate movements that she knew were meant to torture her. Her pussy was so wet and aching, and her nipples were dying to have his mouth and hands on them, sucking, nipping, pinching, pulling. God, but she needed him.

He eased onto the bed at her feet. Her knees were bent and she had been clenching her thighs together just to help ease the ache. He placed his hands on the insides of her knees and pressed them apart, fully exposing her pussy. He smiled and lowered his head and she heard him drawing in his breath, taking in her scent.

Adan's long brown hair swung forward as his mouth neared her folds. The strands trailed over her belly and she gave a soft moan as he nuzzled her mound. Despite herself she gave a whimper of need that all but begged him.

"Okay, I'm sorry already." She arched her hips closer to his face. "Just lick my pussy, please."

It was his turn to chuckle, and she knew he was getting even with her. Paybacks were *definitely* a bitch.

He licked her slit in one long swipe and she couldn't help the cry that escaped her lips. "I'm so damn close already." She squirmed and tried to raise her hips closer to his face. "Not much and I'll be there."

His look was fierce when he met her eyes, and she could tell he was holding himself back from plunging his cock into her. He drove one of his fingers in and out of her pussy while she watched. She gasped as his knuckles pounded against her clit. *Damn* but that felt good.

Just when she was about to climax, Adan eased his finger out of her and she almost sobbed at the loss of contact. He moved up her body until his hands were braced to either side of her chest and he was looking down at her. His cock pressed against her mound—all it would take was a little shift in position and she could bring him right inside of her.

"Finally," she murmured as she grasped his erection.

"Not yet, love." He lowered his head and brushed his lips over her forehead as he removed her hand from his cock. "I am not finished with you yet."

Kara shivered at the low, husky timber of his words. His warm male scent and the feel of his chest rubbing against her nipples magnified her need.

"From the first moment I saw you, I wanted you, Kara." The coarse stubble on his face scraped her cheek as he moved his mouth to her ear and murmured, "I saw the desire in your eyes from the window."

"Yes," she whispered. She couldn't deny that the mere sight of him had sent thrills shooting through her belly straight to her pussy.

He lightly nipped her earlobe. "What about your heart?" He slowly trailed kisses down the curve of her neck. "Have you not felt that we are meant for one another?"

"It's too soon." Kara couldn't identify the feelings she had for Adan, couldn't fathom them. Lust definitely. But love? "Yes, much too soon."

"Mmmm." Adan trailed lazy kisses down her chest, circled her pendant and then licked his way up the curve of one breast. "We shall see."

"Cocky S.O.B.," she muttered and then gasped as Adan's hot mouth latched onto her nipple. "Damn, Adan." She wrapped her arms around his neck and grasped his long, thick hair in her fists.

He alternately licked and suckled her nipples. His stubble chafed her breasts as he lightly nipped each one, causing the most exquisite darts of pain and pleasure that intermingled until the sensations felt as one.

Adan paid the utmost attention to her breasts until her nipples were so sensitive she was sure she could come with just a little more sucking by his hot mouth.

When her body began to tremble with an oncoming climax, Adan moved away, licking a path down the center of her belly, and she grudgingly let his hair slip through her fingers.

"You jerk," she grumbled, and Adan laughed softly.

The closer he came to her pussy, the wetter she became. But after he nuzzled her mound, he moved to the inside of her thigh and gently nipped it.

"Ow, you big lug." It didn't hurt her, instead it turned her on even more. "Please. Please, fuck me now."

"No, love." Adan licked a path to the inside of her knee and then blew his warm breath over the wet skin.

Kara shivered and her thighs trembled. "You're just going to keep doing this to me." A statement, not a question. She knew exactly what he was trying to do to her. Kara clenched the bedcovers in her fists. She was *so* on the edge, but never close enough to achieve what she knew was going to be the orgasm to end all orgasms.

Before she knew what was happening, Adan grabbed her by her hips and flipped her over onto her belly. Kara gave a cry of surprise as she found herself face down, her nose buried in the soft taupe bedcover, her pendant dangling from her throat.

Adan rubbed his palms over his woman's ass and began kneading the firm flesh. By all the stars, she was beautiful. "On your hands and knees," he said.

"Take me now, Adan," Kara demanded as she pushed herself up so that her thighs were wide and the dark pink folds of her pussy were clearly visible.

"That's it, love." Adan's cock was so hard he would surely spew his seed all over Kara's ass if he but rubbed the head of his shaft along the crack of her buttocks. But he was determined to make her wait as long as possible, until neither could take one second more.

Adan moved so that his hips were tight against Kara's. With a moan she pushed back and rubbed her ass against his cock. He almost lost control.

He bent over her back, reached for her breasts and tweaked her nipples. She gave another moan, this time louder and longer.

"Please." Her voice trembled and she sounded close to tears of frustration. "I need you now, Adan."

"Do you need me or my cock, love?" He brushed his lips across her backbone.

Kara shuddered and let out a soft mewling sound. "Not a fair question when you've got me like this." She wiggled her hips and rubbed them against his hardness.

"Whoever said I was fair?" He gripped his erection in his palm and rubbed it against her pussy. "Now tell me what you need."

"You, damn it." Kara arched her back and pressed against him, *hard*.

Adan gripped her hips in his hands. He placed the head of his erection at the entrance to her core and held still for one moment while Kara whimpered. In one hard movement he thrust his cock into her hot pussy.

She cried out at once, her body shuddering with an orgasm so powerful her channel contracted around his erection like a fist squeezing him, almost causing him to climax. He could feel heat rushing through her, heat that came from her crystal.

He gritted his teeth and began plunging in and out of her warmth. He fucked her at a slow and even pace, slamming his hips against her ass.

"You feel so good. Like a sheath made just for me." He increased his pace, driving into her harder and harder. Her cries rang out in time with his thrusts and he felt her body begin to tense, bringing her closer to another orgasm.

"I'm going to come again, Adan." Kara's words came out in a breathy whisper.

"That's it love," he said just as she made a keening sound that stretched out until she cried out long and loud. It seemed that her orgasm would continue forever, and he did not want to stop until she had experienced every bit of pleasure he could give her.

Her arms gave out and she bent her head to the cover. He watched his cock move in and out as he continued to pound into her.

When he couldn't hold back any longer, his climax barreled through him like the mother of all snowstorms.

Chapter Eleven

Three days after his release from the med-room, Adan was almost healed due to the Clans' technology and Ana's medical skills. Snow crunched beneath his and Kara's boots as they walked beside the lake, and he was holding her small hand in his. Even in her snowsuit she looked beautiful, her green eyes bright, her face framed by fur from the hood of her suit.

Adan had tried to bring up the crystal pendant over the past days, but something held him back. He was afraid she would believe he only wanted her for the crystal. But he wanted all of her. Perhaps he was being weak, but he had decided to let the Cwen explain all. T'ni Lael could better tell Kara of the pendant's history and its purpose.

In the distance, children played beside the lake, worked on their ice castles, and had snowball battles between the parapets. Their laughter and chatter warmed his soul, as much as the woman beside him warmed his heart.

Over the past days he had shown her around the village with pride. She had taken in everything with enthusiasm and seemed to especially enjoy visiting the school and watching the children work and play. She even participated in some of their activities, her eyes bright and a smile lighting her face. On more than one occasion, she had expressed how much she missed visiting the children at the orphanage near her home.

Wind chilled their cheeks and snowflakes swirled through the leaded skies while they moved along the lake's snowy bank. One snowflake landed on the tip of Kara's nose and he brought them both to a stop, lowered his head, and kissed it away. She beamed up at him, her smile like a burst of sunshine that brightened everything around them and chased away the gray.

He tugged at her curl and returned her smile. "Having you here with me—it makes my life have meaning again, Kara Marks."

Her eyes widened and her smile dimmed a little. "I don't know that I can stay here, Adan. My life, my friends—"

He placed his finger against her lips. "Shhh, love. A little time. You agreed."

Kara gave a slow nod, her lips brushing over his finger in a way that made his groin tighten and his gut clench.

He dropped his hand away from her face and she said softly, "I know about your wife and child. I'm so sorry."

The surprise at her words sent a ripple through him. Aye, the pain would never completely go away, but it did not hurt nearly as much with Kara by his side.

"Lilli," he said.

"Yes, she told me." The expression on Kara's face was one of caring, and of sorrow for him. "I saw the holo-vids. Your family was beautiful, Adan."

Raising his head he looked to the Mirror Mountains and stared at them for one long moment. In the glittering surface he could almost see Anna's quick grin, and Adam's dimple when he laughed. It seemed only yesterday, yet so long ago.

Before now, thinking about them nearly drove him to his knees. But because of Kara, he found the pain had faded some. He still loved his wife and son, and always would, but now it was time to go on. To go on with Kara.

"I hope you don't mind me saying anything about them." Kara's voice brought his attention back to her. "It was none of my business, I know."

"You have every right." He hooked his finger under her chin and studied her for one long moment. "I miss them both, loved them with all my heart. They will always be a part of me."

"As they should be." Kara's tone and expression held no jealousy, only a hint of sadness for what he had lost.

"Throughout the years, after their deaths, I was angry and bitter. I tucked away my heart, buried my soul. I did not think I could love again," he said, wondering how much more he should say, but finding he could not stop. "Until I met you."

Her green eyes were wide and her lips parted. "Adan…"

A frown creased her features as she turned and stared at something past him. "I thought kids weren't allowed to play on the lake."

Adan's blood chilled as his gaze shot up in time to see a small boy walking onto the ice to retrieve a bright red ball. He was stepping carefully, as if aware the ice was dangerous, but seemed determined to go after his toy.

"Keiden!" Adan shouted and tore away from Kara. "Do not move!" Behind him he heard Kara's breath coming out in small pants, her boots making soft crunching sounds against the snow as she chased after him.

The little boy bent over to pick up the ball.

"Keiden!" Adan belted out again.

The child picked up the ball and froze when he saw Adan running toward him. "I just wanted to get my ball," he said, panic in his small voice, as if knowing he was in trouble.

"Do not move," Adan repeated as he came up to the lakeshore. Kara stopped beside him.

A loud crack echoed through the chill air.

Adan's heart stopped.

Everyone and everything around them went quiet.

A woman's scream ripped through the silence, "Keiden!"

The boy's lower lip trembled. "I want my mom."

"I will take you to your mother." Adan stepped to the edge of the ice. He was a little more than an arm's length from the boy. "Hold still."

Another crack. Ice jerked beneath Keiden's feet and his eyes went wide with terror.

Adan knelt beside the ice. In the background he heard the boy's mother sobbing, heard other Clan members trying to calm her.

"Is there anything I can do?" Kara asked, her voice quivering.

He reached out to Keiden, stretching out his arm as far as he could. Inches still separated them.

Keeping his hand stretched out, Adan eyed the ice at his knees. A crack ran from the shore to where the boy stood. If Adan knelt on it, likely it would give way before he could grasp Keiden's hand.

"You will need to reach for me." Adan's gaze met the boy's terrified eyes. "Slowly."

Keiden shook his head.

Adan tried to stretch himself out further. "You can do it. Your mother has told me how proud she is of you and how strong you are."

Still clinging to his red ball, the child bit his lip.

Another crack. The ice jolted again.

Keiden reached his small hand out and clasped Adan's hand. A moment of relief filled Adan as he started to guide the boy toward him, slowly.

The ice gave way.

A woman screamed.

Fear rocketed through Adan as he tried to jerk Keiden toward him.

The boy plunged through the small crack that had opened in the lake's surface. Keiden screamed as his body wedged between the thick sheets of ice, stopping at his armpits.

Adan tried to pull the boy out, but his small form was trapped, as if between the jaws of a vise.

"I want my mom," Keiden cried out, tears rolling down his face.

"I will get you to your mother," Adan said with determination.

Kara had never been so frightened as she was at that moment. Even when she and Adan had been captured, she had not feared for her life as she feared for this boy's life.

"The ice is freezing around him." Adan tossed a look over his shoulder, never relaxing his hold on the boy. "Get Dominik."

"It will be too late," the boy's mother wailed. "He'll freeze to death."

Kara's fear nearly overwhelmed her. The heat of the pendant began pulsing through her and she remembered what she had done at the ice palace. Could she do the same here?

She didn't take time to think about it any longer. She focused on the ice around Keiden's waist. Concentrating on the energy within her pendant, she imagined it melting the lake's surface.

Adan was shouting. Keiden was crying. His mother was screaming.

Kara blanked them all out.

The heat of the pendant roared through her and burst from her in a hot wave. Ice cracked. Melted before her eyes.

Keiden's body came free. Adan stumbled back, jerking the boy from the lake at the same time. He landed on his backside, with Keiden in his arms.

Kara dropped to her knees, her breathing heavy, her heart pounding in her throat. Around her were shouts and a flurry of movement. Keiden was bundled and taken away.

The next thing she knew, Adan had his arms wrapped around her, and was kissing her forehead. "Thank you, my love," he murmured as he held her tight. "Thank you."

* * * * *

Holding Kara's hand, Adan led her through the hallways to the enormous common room. No matter that he truly did not want to share her, he looked forward to introducing her to more of his people.

"I'm nervous." Kara held her hand to her belly as she looked up at him. Her pink sarong floated around her body and defined her attributes. "What if your people don't like me? Don't want me here?"

"How could they not?" He paused in mid-step and brought her to him. "Even if you had not saved Keiden's life yesterday, we would welcome you as one of our own."

"You saved him," she argued yet again. "My pendant only helped a little."

"Enough." He ruffled his fingers through her curls. "No more arguing over it. You saved the boy's life and that is what matters."

"I don't belong here, Adan." In a nervous gesture, she ran her free palm down the soft material of her sarong.

He lightly brushed his lips over hers, breathing in her scent of spring and woman. When he raised his head he squeezed her hand. "You belong here as much as I do."

She didn't respond, but gave him a little smile. It was enough to warm his heart and his loins, and he almost turned them around and headed back to their room, to take her hard and fast.

Before they reached the common room, laughter and music filtered out to meet them.

"What's going on?" Kara asked.

"Once a month many of the Clans' members gather for a night of dancing, good food and mugs of fire ale." Adan brought her up to the open archway where they could see his people dancing to music played by Dane and two other knights. Dane was highly skilled at an old Earth instrument called an acoustic guitar. He composed countless songs that he played for the Clans when various members pressed him.

It surprised Kara to see the dangerous-looking man playing the guitar for a roomful of people. She would never have guessed the brooding knight was an artist. "He's *good.*"

"Aye, that he is." Adan tugged her hand and pulled her through the doorway and into the throng.

"What he's playing—it sounds like rock music, but not," she said, raising her voice over the laughing, the chatter, and the music. The mood in the room was infectious, and Kara couldn't help but smile.

Adan smiled in return, and began introducing her to Clan members, many of whom hugged and kissed her, thanking her for saving Keiden's life. The boy's mother was the most profuse in her gratitude. She promised them that Keiden was doing very well and would be in school the following day.

Some of the women were dressed like Kara, in sarongs of various hues. Others wore the knight's uniform and bore the Blackstar sword and star emblem on their sleeves. Many of the men also wore the uniform, and others were dressed in more casual shirts, pants and boots. The people seemed happy and carefree for the most part, at least tonight.

Adan introduced her to so many people that her head began to spin. She had an unusually good memory for names and faces, so at least in that regard she was in luck.

She saw Lilli in the arms of a gorgeous dark-haired man who was apparently *very* familiar with her. Lilli was rubbing the man's crotch through his pants, and one of her breasts was free from her sarong as he played with her nipple. *In full view of everyone in the room.* Kara's eyes widened when Adan took her directly up to the couple and introduced the man as the third Clan Leader, Dominik. She had heard about him from Adan, but had yet to meet him.

"Welcome to Blackstar." Dominik took her hand and kissed the inside of her wrist. He flicked his tongue over her flesh, causing Kara to shiver.

"Er, my pleasure." Kara pulled away from him, trying not to look at Lilli's exposed breast and hoping no one noticed the rise of her own nipples.

Adan scowled and Dominik gave him a teasing grin. He lowered his head and began to suck Lilli's nipple just before Kara and Adan started to walk away.

Kara swallowed back the feeling of lust rising up within her, and tried to ignore the tingling in her pussy. "Is Lilli his wife?" she said over the noise in the room.

Adan lowered his head and spoke near her ear where she could hear. "Lilli is a pleasure-partner. She enjoys pleasure with any man who needs to ease the fire in his loins."

Kara's eyes widened. "She's a prostitute?"

He frowned and shook his head. "No. It is simply something she has chosen to do, something she enjoys very much."

"Oh." Kara tried to imagine being a pleasure-partner and fucking a variety of men. It kind of turned her on—even though she couldn't imagine herself with anyone but Adan. And then another thought occurred to her. "Have you 'relieved your needs' with Lilli?"

Adan shrugged and continued leading her through the crowd. By his lack of denial, she knew he had. The thought sent a fierce rush of jealousy through her, and she wanted to slug him.

What was wrong with her? It wasn't like he belonged to her or something.

As they moved through the dancers, Kara caught more people making out along the fringes. Bare breasts, hard nipples, naked backsides, mouths sucking erections, and fingers stroking clits. Apparently sex was something these people didn't think belonged only in the bedroom. Who knew, maybe there would be a mass orgy tonight.

Even though the idea was titillating, that wasn't something she was prepared to deal with, or be involved in. She was a one-man woman and she didn't like to share.

When Dane finished playing a set, Adan presented her to him. This time the man was much more gracious, but he still had that hard look in his eyes, as if he found it difficult to trust anyone.

While the music was stopped, many Clan members mingled, some continued their sexual play, while others ate from an interesting-looking buffet.

A beautiful woman approached Kara and Adan, causing Adan to look very uncomfortable. Kara's pendant gave a surprising burst of warmth.

"Cwen," Adan said as the woman came to a stop in front of them. "As always, it is a pleasure to see you."

Kara had heard Adan speak of the woman who had survived the Ice-Witch's attack, along with the remnants of the Sanor realm, but had never met her. To Kara's surprise she was beautiful. She looked like she was in her thirties, rather than ancient as Kara had imagined.

The Cwen's waist-length hair spilled over her emerald green-robed shoulders as she inclined her head toward Adan. Her blonde hair was in ringlets not unlike Kara's, but much longer. Her skin was almost as pale as the ice-ghosts', as if she rarely saw the light of day.

"Clan Leader Valnez." The Cwen's words were thickly accented and she spoke in halting English.

The woman fixed her gaze on Kara. "My child." She held her palms out and took Kara's hands in her own, pulling her away from Adan. "It has been so long. Far too long." Moisture glistened in the Cwen's green eyes.

Kara was almost too surprised to speak. "Too long for what?"

Adan cleared his throat and the Cwen moved her gaze to his. Something silent seemed to pass between them, and the woman nodded. She turned her smile back to Kara, only this time it looked almost strained. "I must be going. I will return in a week's time and hope to have a greater opportunity to spend time with you."

"Uh, sure," Kara said, and watched as the Cwen turned and slipped through the crowd like mist through trees.

Kara glanced up at Adan. "What was *that* all about?"

The music started up again, a slower paced tune, and Adan brought her into the circle of his arms. "I simply want to be alone with you, love."

She smiled as she laid her head against his chest and wrapped her arms around his waist, enjoying the feel of his powerful embrace as they swayed. For a while she lost touch with reality. All that she was aware of was him. His intensely masculine smell, the way his hard muscles flexed beneath her cheek, the feel of his thighs pressed to hers. And his cock—lord, his very hard erection pressed against her belly.

He nuzzled her neck, his stubble scraping her sensitive skin and his tongue licking a trail of fire as he moved to her ear. He bit at her earlobe and she gasped at the erotic sensation. "You are so beautiful, Kara."

She gave a soft moan as he moved his lips along her jawline to the corner of her mouth. He traced her lips with his tongue, and then lightly nipped at her lower lip, causing her to give a soft cry. Her nipples ached where they pressed against his chest, and her thighs grew damp from where her juices moistened them. He was sure to catch her scent, to know how much he turned her on.

Adan's hands roamed her curves, sending chills through her as his fingers skimmed the one side of her that was bared from the sarong. She wanted him to remove the clip and let the soft material settle around her feet like a frothy cloud that she could dance upon. "Fuck me, Adan," she said with a moan. "Fuck me."

Something nudged her backside, and Kara startled out of her trance. She tore her mouth from Adan's and came back to reality. They were still in the common room, and another pair of dancers had just bumped into them. Her cheeks burned as she realized that she had been ready to strip right here and now, in a roomful of people. Not that anyone would notice, considering what was going on around them.

Her gaze shot to Adan's and he gave her an unrepentant grin. Somehow he knew she'd lost all sense of place and time. He grasped her hand and led her through the crowd, barely acknowledging the people who greeted him on their way out the door.

They slipped into the hallway and her heart pounded with excitement as she hurried to keep up with him. Adan rounded a corner and practically yanked her into a recessed hallway. Before she had a chance to catch her breath, his hands were in her curls and he captured her mouth in a kiss so hard and deep that she grew dizzy from its potency.

She could still hear the beat of the music throbbing from the common room, as her pussy throbbed for Adan. He pushed her hard against the wall and she clung to him as she wrapped her legs around his waist.

Their kiss grew deeper, their moans louder as they ravished each other. Kara's pendant pulsed heat through her, hotter and hotter yet. He grasped the clip of her sarong and she heard the sound of material ripping and the clatter of metal upon the floor. Her sarong dropped to her waist, baring her breasts, and his shirt abraded her nipples.

Adan jerked up the skirt of her sarong so that all her clothing was around her waist, and she felt cool air over her ass and mound. He grasped one of her thighs and his thumb found her clit. Kara gasped and cried out as he broke the kiss and rubbed harder against the tight nub.

"That's it, love." Adan's eyes were dark with passion. "Take it, take it all."

"Jeez, Adan." Kara clung to his shoulders, squirming from the intense sensation. "Someone could see us. Hear us."

"Would you like that, Kara?" he asked as he thrust one finger inside her channel while he continued rubbing her clit with his thumb. "Would you like people staring as I make you come?"

The mere idea of being watched brought her closer to peak. Her thighs began to tremble and she dug her fingernails into his shoulders.

"That's it," he murmured as he lowered his head and licked her nipple. "Come for me, love, and then I will fuck you right here, for any and all to see."

At his words, at the image of him fucking her up against the wall, a shower of warmth rushed through Kara, heating her from head to toe. Wild sensations expanded from her nipples to her belly to her pussy and she bit her lip hard to keep from screaming.

Adan continued thumbing her clit and licking her nipples as her body jerked against his hand. The coppery taste of blood touched her tongue, she had bitten her lip so hard. She smelled her own juices, felt perspiration dampening her skin. The wall was hard against her back and his shoulders taut beneath her nails as her orgasm broke in wave after wave beneath his skilled fingers.

When he finally stopped, he took her mouth again in a fiery kiss. In the background Kara heard the sound of voices approaching the passageway they were in, feminine laughter and a man's low seductive voice. Tremors rippled through Kara, knowing that they could be caught so easily.

Adan didn't even wait until the couple had passed before he pulled away from their kiss and released his hold on her with one hand long enough to unfasten his pants. His cock sprang out, the head brushing the curls of her pussy and Adan hissed with pleasure.

He kissed her again, driving his tongue into her mouth at the same time he drove his cock into her pussy. At the feel of him filling her so intensely, so completely, Kara practically screamed with pleasure into his mouth.

With deep, slow thrusts he began to fuck her, his balls slapping against her pussy, the hair around his cock pressing into the curls of her mound. He felt so good, so big, filling her with every movement he made. She loved how he easily held her while fucking her up against the wall. He was so strong, so commanding.

He tore his mouth from hers and looked down, and she followed his gaze to see his length moving in and out of her. His shaft glistened with her juices and it looked long and thick as he continued his thrusts.

"I love to see my cock inside you," he said as he watched them join and rejoin. "I love making you mine in every way."

Kara could only groan and keep her eyes fixed on the two of them. His words, his body, his scent—it was all so overwhelming, and so, so good.

The soft material of her sarong felt and looked erotic bunched up around her waist. Her breasts bounced with every pump of his hips, and the sound of flesh slapping flesh was loud enough that she was afraid someone passing by would hear—although that thought rather added to the thrill of the moment.

Another storm whirled within her, from pussy to nipples, from limb to limb. She looked up from where they were joined and met Adan's fierce dark eyes. "Hold on, love," he said, much lower now. "I'm going to fuck you like you've never been fucked before."

The storm inside her zinged with lightning from his mere words. She clung to him as he pressed her hard against the wall and began pummeling his hips against her pussy. The storm grew and grew, a maelstrom of feelings, of sensations, of sounds. Her blood thundered in her ears, throbbed in her veins. She couldn't take her eyes from

Adan's, his dark gaze reflecting back the storm raging in his own body, his own soul.

Her orgasm slammed into her with hurricane force. This time she tilted her head back and screamed, long and loud, like the fierce winds of a tropical storm. She had never screamed during sex, ever. But she couldn't help it as wave after wave after wave of tremors wracked her body. In the far, far distance she heard Adan's shout, felt the throb of his cock in her pussy, and the warmth of his come filling her.

When she finally came down from the very peaks of the waves, she realized that Adan was holding her tight, her head pressed to his chest. The thunder she heard now was the pounding of his heart beneath her ear.

Chapter Twelve

Adan strode into the small school, knowing he would find Kara there. While she had been on Blackstar, she had taken to assisting the teacher in the early primers' classroom while he dealt with Clan matters—and the impending attack by the Ice-Witch's warriors.

He pushed thoughts of battle away and allowed thoughts of Kara to fill his mind. His boots echoed in the silent hallway as he headed to the youngest students' classroom. No doubt Kara would be helping the children with their crafts. She had surprised him with her talent for craft-making, and she had taught the students how to design many projects.

When he reached the classroom he paused in the doorway and hitched one shoulder against the doorframe. His gaze sought Kara out and found her sitting at one of the small tables, clad in a modest crimson sarong. Her head was bent and her curls obscured her eyes while she showed a small girl how to make a collage. Kara focused her attention solely on the child, and she spoke soft words of approval as the girl glued a piece of material to the paper.

Adan's heart swelled with pride and love for his woman while he watched her with the girl. He could picture her with their own daughter, and it surprised him. When his wife and child had died on Earth, he had been certain he would never love again, would never have another child.

He had come to truly appreciate all of Kara's qualities, and that only magnified his love for her. She was intelligent, passionate about her beliefs and she interacted well with his people. So much so that he already felt she was a part of the Clan. He only hoped she felt the same.

"It's Clan Leader Valnez!" Keiden shouted as he spotted Adan in the doorway.

To Adan's astonishment, the five year old bolted out of his seat and ran straight for Adan, wrapping his arms around Adan's knees. Before he had time to register that, the whole class of fifteen students had surrounded him, chattering while they hugged him and virtually hung off him.

Adan reached down and swung Keiden up so that they were face-to-face. The boy looked so much like Adan's dead son that a lump rose up in his throat.

His voice was rough as he said, "Can you tell me what in the stars' names is going on here?"

Keiden pointed to Kara. "Ms. Marks told us that you need lots of hugs."

Adan's gaze met Kara's and she sported an impish grin.

"I see." Adan set the boy down and ruffled his hair. "Back to your seats everyone."

The children laughed and scampered back to their desks. Chairs scraped across the floor as they pulled their seats up and their laughter died away. The teacher, Mrs. Night, an elderly — and quite often grumpy — teacher, just shook her head and went back to working with the students on their projects.

Adan's gaze focused on Kara and he strode to the back of the classroom. She bit her lower lip and he could tell she was holding back a laugh.

When he reached her he took her hand and pulled her to her feet. "What was that all about, woman?"

She caught her breath and her nipples puckered beneath her sarong. "Maybe we should discuss this in private."

Without saying another word, Adan tightened his grip on her hand and pulled her through the classroom and toward the door.

"Bye, Ms. Marks," Keiden yelled and Mrs. Night immediately reprimanded him.

When they were alone in the hallway, Adan pulled Kara roughly to him, and he felt the heat of her pendant between them. "I need hugs, do I?"

She grinned and wrapped her arms around his neck. "Most definitely."

Adan cupped the back of her head and brought her to him in a rough kiss. How he loved this woman. He couldn't get enough of her.

Her mouth was soft and sweet and he reveled in the taste of her. His cock sprang to life and he knew he needed to be inside her now.

Kara's mind whirled with the depth of Adan's kiss. He filled her in so many ways that she could no longer imagine life without him. Yet could she turn her back on her home, her life on Earth of the past?

When Adan pulled away from her, he looked at her with that soul-deep gaze that always took her breath away.

"Come," he said in a low growl as he released his hold on her hair and took her hand again.

A thrill ran from her nipples to her pussy and her heartbeat accelerated as Adan led her through the school's hallways and into the Clans' common room. She was so anxious to be with him that the skirt of her sarong nearly tangled around her legs.

They had to cross through the busy room, and Adan barely acknowledged greetings from his people. Kara would have laughed at his single-mindedness, if she wasn't so horny herself. She couldn't wait to get to their bedroom.

Their bedroom.

She swallowed back the sudden rise of nervousness. Such a short time knowing this man, and she was thinking of them as a couple — as if this was permanent.

Would it be? Could she make that decision?

Just as they made it through the crowd and into another hallway, Adan came to an abrupt stop. Kara saw the Cwen, the woman she had met at the Clans' celebration, and for some strange reason her pendant felt even hotter against her chest than it had the last time.

"Cwen." Adan said with a slight bow of his head. Kara knew by the tightening of Adan's hand around hers that he was not happy at being waylaid when he wanted to be alone with her.

"Clan Leader Valnez." The Cwen nodded in return. "I have given you the week you asked for."

Kara frowned.

The Sanor queen turned to Kara and smiled. "My child."

"Hi." Kara felt a stirring of nervousness in her belly. "Why do you keep calling me your child?"

"Have you not realized it yet?" The Cwen looked somewhat surprised. "You are a child of Sanor. You were sent to Earth with the crystal to protect you both."

Kara stared at the woman as the words hit her. They didn't quite sink in, more like bounced off and ricocheted around the hallway.

"Yeah, right." Kara shook her head. "You're messing with me."

"Come with me." The Cwen released Kara, turned, and walked away. Adan grasped Kara's hand in his. She looked up at him to see his jaw set.

"What does she mean?" Kara whispered to Adan as they followed the Cwen. "Is she delusional or something?"

He gave a slow shake of his head. "We shall find out."

They reached a room guarded by two of Adan's warriors. She recognized the Blackstar sword and star insignia on their black jumpsuits. The warriors stepped aside and let the three of them pass.

They entered a room that had a panoramic window with a beautiful view of Crystal Valley. The floors and walls were made of wood, the walls inlaid with precious gemstones from the mines.

In the center of the room was a large wooden conference table with several high-backed chairs scattered around it. In one corner stood a strange arch, from which a humming sound came. The arch was beautiful with runes around it similar to the ones on Adan's sword. The lettering glowed a soft gold, too.

When the Cwen came to a stop and turned to face them, Adan released Kara's hand and said, "Explain," in a tone so curt it surprised her. "What does Kara mean to Sanor?"

Apparently his tone surprised the Cwen, too. She raised an eyebrow. "I told you the crystal was hidden with a most valuable treasure, and that you would need your heart and soul to find both."

Kara's gaze darted from the Cwen's to Adan's.

His features softened when his gaze met Kara's. "Aye," he said softly. "I found the most precious of treasures."

Kara brought her hand up to her pendant which was burning hotter than normal. Her thoughts whirred. She couldn't believe the Cwen's statement that she belonged here. And what was this priceless treasure Adan supposedly retrieved with the crystal? A part of her knew what they were going to say, but another part wanted to reject it right off. She needed to hear it, needed to know what was happening.

She took a deep breath. "One of you had better tell me, in plain English, what the hell is going on."

The Cwen gave one slow nod. "I am T'ni Lael of the Sanor realm. I am your mother."

Kara's jaw dropped.

Adan gave a grunt of surprise.

For one endless moment, Kara just stared at the woman. Details suddenly stood out that she had only casually noticed before. The Cwen's blonde corkscrew curls, and green eyes almost the same shade as Kara's. Even the Cwen's features were somewhat similar. Her small nose and the determined set of her jaw.

Somehow Kara didn't question it. She knew it was true—she was from Sanor and this woman was her mother.

Kara spoke the first thought that came to her lips. "You abandoned me."

"Yes, and no, child." T'ni Lael gave a pained expression. "I did leave you, but it was to save you."

Fire burned in Kara's gut. She had spent her life being passed from one foster home to the next, never truly feeling like she was wanted. Never knowing what it was like to have a *family*.

Her fury boiled over, and her words came out harsh and fast. "Do you have any idea what it's like to think your parents didn't want you and to be shuffled from one family to another? Do you have any idea what my life has been like?"

"I have questioned my decision every day." T'ni Lael sighed and her green eyes glistened as if with unshed tears. "I did what was necessary to protect the crystal and you."

Anger burned hot and bright within Kara and she grabbed the crystal in her hand, wanting to yank it off and throw it across the room. "So you figured it was perfectly fine to abandon me. Well, maybe I was better off growing up a nobody than having a mother who cares more about this damn crystal than me."

The Cwen's shoulders drooped and she seemed saddened by Kara's outburst. "You do not know how important the *L'sen* Crystal is, Kara. You do not know how important you are to us. Both you and the crystal will change all our lives for the better."

"Fuck you." Kara whirled on her bare heel and marched out of the room, past the two guards. She clenched her fists at her side and gritted her teeth so hard she thought they'd crack.

She heard Adan's boots thump against the wooden flooring, but she didn't slow down.

Adan, of course, caught up in mere strides, and grasped her elbow. He didn't say anything, simply walked with her through the halls and to their chambers.

There she went again, thinking *their chambers*, like they were a permanent couple.

Kara wasn't sure she wanted Adan's company right now. She felt used by everyone around her, and she wasn't sure what to think.

Nothing was as it seemed. From the time she'd met Adan until the moment she'd learned the Cwen was her mother, her world had been continuously stirred, flipped, shaken, and mashed. Her pendant hadn't been some kind of benign piece of glass, and Adan had been searching for that pendant when he found her. Now, she'd just found out that she had been sent from this world and abandoned on Earth, and her mother was still alive. What else could happen?

When they reached the bedchamber Adan placed his hand to the ID screen. The door slid up and allowed them entrance, then closed behind them.

Before Kara could turn on Adan and yell at him, he had her in his arms and held her tight so that her cheek was to his chest, her body firmly against his.

"I had no idea, love." He kissed the top of her hair and Kara felt herself begin to melt. "Yet, I cannot say I would have done any different. You belong here, in my arms."

"Do I?" She tilted her head to look at him. "I don't know anything for certain right now. My whole life has been turned upside down over the past weeks and I just don't know how to deal with it."

Adan pressed her head against his chest again and squeezed her tighter. "You can count on one thing for certain. And that is my love." He moved away and hooked his finger under her chin and tilted her head up so that she was looking at him. "I love you, Kara. I do not care about the damned powercrystal. We could put it in the time-arch and send it far, far away, to another galaxy, another place and time. To a sun where it might burn to ash. As long as I have you, that is all that matters."

With all her heart, Kara knew Adan spoke the truth. He was an honest man, a good man. She had seen it in his day-to-day dealings with his people, and in how they responded to him. Even though he had a gruff exterior, it was obvious he loved his Clan members and that they loved him.

And she had seen it in how he treated her. As if she was a princess, someone he cherished and loved.

At that very moment, as she stared up into his dark eyes, Kara realized she was in love with Adan. There was no doubt about it now. She loved everything about him.

But she wasn't sure what that meant yet. She needed time to sort everything out.

Adan brought his head down and brushed his lips over hers. Kara sighed, some of her frustration and hurt easing out of her body as she turned her focus completely over to Adan. At this moment, he was all that mattered in this world. She'd worry about everything else later.

Right now she wanted him more than anything. And she didn't want slow lovemaking. She wanted sex, hard and fierce.

Kara flung her arms around Adan's neck and kissed him with all her pent up passion. His body tensed and his cock grew rigid against her belly. With a low growl of approval, his tongue plunged in and out of her mouth, mating with hers, as rough and hard as she wanted him to fuck her. She wrapped her legs around his waist and climbed him, never breaking the kiss.

He carried her to the table and placed Kara upon it, next to the star sculpture. She tore his mouth from his and gasped for air. "Damn, Adan. I need you."

"I always need you." He held her with one hand while his other found the shoulder clasp on her sarong. He fumbled with it, then ripped it off and flung it away. Two ruined sarongs now, but she really didn't care. The gauzy material slipped over her breasts, the silken feel a contrast to the rough man before her.

Kara moaned with pleasure as his mouth found her nipples and she cried out as he nipped each one. Damn that felt so, so good. While he sucked her tight nubs, he pressed her legs apart and ground his cloth-covered cock against her pussy.

He released her long enough to unfasten his pants and push her sarong up over her hips, palming her ass. "I have been dying to fuck you all day, love," he said, rubbing the head of his erection over her folds.

He slid in a fraction and she tried to slide closer to him, but he held her too tightly. "You are always so hot, wet, and ready for me."

"Dammit, Adan!" she cried out, but he only guided her down, so that she was flat on her back on the table.

He plunged his cock into her pussy. She cried out at the feel of his incredible length inside of her. His obsidian gaze remained locked on her face as he began to fuck her hard. There was no taking it slow now; he was taking her with wild, possessive strokes.

The table rubbed against her back, her breasts bouncing up and down. Adan's pants rubbed against her pussy while he thrust into her, stimulating her even more. He slammed into her harder and harder and vaguely she felt the star sculpture tumble over, heard a crash, and the sound of glass breaking.

Sweat rolled down his face and the smell of his male musk amplified her desire. Kara felt her orgasm building and building, until she couldn't hold back any longer. Her thighs began to tremble around Adan's waist and she tried to rise up. He placed his hand on her belly, pushing her harder against the table and drove into her even faster.

"Tell me you'll stay Kara," he demanded.

"Adan!" Kara shouted as her climax burned her like lava bursting from a volcano. Heat flushed over her from her pendant, sending fire from her head to her toes. Her orgasm continued in multiple aftershocks while Adan fucked her.

With a savage growl, Adan came. She felt his cock throb within her pussy, felt the heat of him spilling inside her.

Her body went limp as she collapsed, her arms and legs still wrapped around him, his cock still inside her.

"Okay," she murmured. "I'll stay...at least a while longer."

Chapter Thirteen

The spybug zipped from a snowtree, closer to the tower where Echna and her ice-ghost commanders were meeting yet again. They had been spending a great deal of time there over the past three weeks, ever since Adan and Kara had escaped.

Adan frowned while he focused on the view screen, as the Ice-Witch strode across her courtyard and vanished into the tower. What was she up to now? He had no doubt she would retaliate for the loss of the crystal and for the loss of the warriors that had been in the ship that his men had destroyed. He would be doing the same, preparing his own knights for attack and retribution.

However the Ice-Witch's warriors far outnumbered Adan's knights. It would take great cunning and skill to fight off an invasion by the ice-ghosts. His knights were prepared, their swords sharpened for hand-to-hand combat, their laser weapons primed for battle. The numerous Clans' ships were at the ready, and guardcraft continually monitored the borders.

Yet the ice-ghosts had not attacked. Adan rubbed his stubbled jaw as his gaze sought out any clue that might be hidden in the snowbound landscape.

Nothing.

He had no doubt Echna would attack before the sun filtered through the planet's natural shield, on *L'sen*, when the sun was at its strongest. It was the one day every two decades that snow would actually melt, and sunlight would glint off the Mirror Mountains as if they were made of countless diamonds.

That was when she had attacked two decades ago, forcing the people of Sanor to abandon their attempt at change. They had barely kept the pendant and the babe — Kara — from Echna's hands by sending them through the time-arch.

At least the Ice-Witch would be unable to use her magical powers to travel directly into the village — the Clans' powershield saw to that. But attacking via the borders was another story. No matter how keenly his knights patrolled the borders, the ice-ghosts would be able to attack.

According to the Cwen and her meticulous records, this second decade was the one time that the power of the *L'sen* Crystal would merge with the power of the Tower of Light and the sun, and change all their fortunes.

What the Ice-Witch wanted with the crystal, Adan wasn't certain. He knew only what T'ni Lael had explained — that the witch would wield incredible power that would destroy Adan's Clans.

Adan slammed his fist on the desk then commanded the view screen off. He would do whatever it took to protect his people, even if it meant outright war with the Ice-Witch.

He pushed himself out of the chair and strode toward the travel chamber where he was to meet with Dane and Dominik. But instead of focusing on the meeting ahead, Adan's thoughts returned to Kara and their lovemaking of the night before. The tightness in his belly dissipated at the memory and a smile curved the corner of his mouth. She hadn't promised to stay for long, but nevertheless, he didn't plan to let her go.

* * * * *

Forcing herself to sit still, Kara perched on the edge of her seat in the guarded travel chamber. The time-arch hummed in the corner, its symbols glowing in tandem with the swirling of her pendant.

Kara sat at the wooden meeting table, facing the Cwen, T'ni Lael.

Her mother.

The woman who'd abandoned her on Earth just to protect a stupid crystal. Kara kept trying to ignore the fact that the Cwen said it was to protect her, too.

Kara clenched her teeth as the pale beauty folded her hands on top of the table. The only reason she was meeting T'ni Lael was because Adan had asked her to, as a favor to him. And where he was concerned, Kara couldn't say no. Except for staying on this planet—she wasn't sure she could spend her life away from all that she had known since she had been abandoned on a family's doorstep as a toddler.

T'ni Lael—Kara refused to truly think of her as "Mother"—gave a serene smile as her green eyes met Kara's.

"You have become a fine young woman," the Cwen said in her thickly accented voice. When Kara didn't respond, the woman added, "I am most proud of you."

Kara's pendant burned hot against her chest and her gaze narrowed. "I don't know what I'm supposed to say to you. I'm not going to pretend everything is all right, because it's not. So why don't we just get this over with and you tell me whatever it is you have to tell me."

T'ni Lael sighed, a long drawn-out sound that hinted at sadness. "I had hoped this meeting would be a joyous one."

Kara folded her arms across her chest and leaned back in her seat. "You thought wrong."

With a slow nod, T'ni Lael said, "I am sorry to hear this." The woman pushed back her chair, stood, and began pacing the wooden flooring, her long emerald green robes trailing behind her. She offered no more apologies, only seemed to accept that Kara didn't wish to form any kind of relationship with her "mother".

That pissed Kara off even more.

"The crystal you wear is very powerful," the Cwen said, her hands steepled as she paced.

"I gathered that." Anger boiling up inside her, Kara folded her arms tighter across her chest. She felt the heat of her pendant grow stronger through her sarong and a flash of concern replaced her anger. She might not like this woman, but she didn't want to burn a hole through her. She took a deep breath and forced herself to relax.

T'ni Lael eyed the crystal as if she was aware of Kara's anger and the stirring of its power. "The crystal was a gift to the Sanor realm from a far advanced people of another world, the Bellen. We were dying even then in this fierce climate, and the crystal was to save our people by changing this world that we call 'Y'chi', but you know as Blackstar. It would have taken Y'chi back to what it once was, countless centuries ago."

Kara frowned, but concentrated on T'ni Lael's words.

"The Bellen also left us the Tower of Light." The woman gestured to the window and Kara's eyes followed to where the monolith stood, glinting in what little true sunlight pierced Blackstar's natural shield.

"One day every second decade, the sun is at its strongest." T'ni Lael's restless pacing let Kara know that the Cwen wasn't as serene as the expression on her face. "On that day, the crystal," the woman continued, "will combine its power with the Tower of Light and turn this ice-planet into a paradise beyond imagination."

Kara allowed the information to sink in. It sounded improbable, but hell, most of what she'd experienced over the last month since she'd met Adan was improbable.

"So you're talking about this crystal having a sort of genesis effect," Kara murmured, thinking of an old movie she saw long ago. She could easily imagine this ice-world as green and lush. Her eyes met T'ni Lael's, eyes that were so like her own. "Wouldn't the snow melt and cause floods?"

"This very same power was used on other ice-planets," the Cwen said. "In each instance the water from the snow seeped into the ground forming reservoirs that continued to give life to the people and the planets' vegetation."

"What happened?" Despite herself, Kara was fascinated by what the Cwen was telling her. "Why wasn't this done before now?"

"The pendant and tower were only gifted to us by the Bellen a little over two decades ago. Unbeknownst to us, the Bellen had kept a close eye on our planet and noted that the planet warmed once every twenty years, enough to use the *L'sen* Crystal and the Tower of Light.

"Before we had a chance to use them, the Ice-Witch attacked, wiping out most of our military and forcing the survivors into the caverns below." T'ni Lael's knuckles whitened, betraying her anger. "We have lived there since, waiting for the time when we could once again attempt to alter the course of our destinies. To bring this world back to what it once was."

Kara narrowed her gaze. "This was once a green planet?"

"Yes," T'ni Lael replied. "A meteor slammed into this world centuries ago, and over time our weather changed. Some of the plants, animals, and trees adapted. But most did not. We are left with ice and cold when once there was spring and beauty."

Kara narrowed her brows in concentration. "How do you know this?"

"The people of Sanor have always kept meticulous records." T'ni Lael's feet barely made a sound as she paced back and forth. "We have kept these cherished items for time on end. They were among what little we saved from the invasion by Echna two decades ago, when we were forced to abandon our lives above ground. We have lived in the caves beneath this village ever since, living on fish and roots."

What a life that would be, to be forced to live underground. Kara could understand why they wanted the world to be what it once was. It truly didn't seem possible, but she knew the technology of alien races could be amazingly advanced. "The sun won't be any closer, so how will this change be sustained?"

"In truth, it will not bring the sun any closer to us, but it will be unnecessary." The Cwen relaxed her hands and brushed one over the folds of her emerald cloak. "The heat generated from the *L'sen* will gather below the planet's natural shield. The shield will hold the heat in, creating a tropical atmosphere that will neither be too warm or too cold."

Kara pictured a mass transformation, something like a nuclear bomb spreading over thousands of miles. "Are you sure this process won't hurt anyone?"

T'ni Lael shook her head. "According to the vids presented by the Bellen, the power of *L'sen* only affects atmosphere and vegetation. It will take months, years even, to fully develop into the world we wish it to be."

"But that's nothing compared to the normal workings of time," Kara added softly.

"You understand now, why we need the crystal?" T'ni Lael asked.

"I suppose so." Her mind wandered for a moment, and she asked the next question that popped into her mind. "What about dear old Dad? I assume I had a father."

The woman nodded. "He was a fine man. He died during the Ice-Witch's attack. It would please you to know that he would not have approved of sending you away."

Kara fixed her gaze on T'ni Lael's green eyes that were so similar to her own. "So *you* sent me with the crystal to protect it until you needed it again."

"And to protect you," she replied softly.

Kara waved off the woman's response. "I'm sure anyone could use the damn thing. It just needs to be at the right place at the right time."

The older woman tilted her head and regarded Kara. "You always had an affinity for the crystal. It warmed whenever it neared you, the power within it only stirred when you held it." She glanced at the crystal on Kara's chest. "See how it responds to your emotions?"

Kara looked down to see the black and silver of the crystal swirling like a phallic-shaped galaxy of stars. It swirled slower now that she wasn't feeling as angry as she had been before. "So you were going to use me as a baby?"

"I am not certain." The Cwen gave a slight shrug of her delicate shoulders. "I could have attempted it, but once we were attacked we missed the one opportunity we had for decades, and I had you sent to Earth of the past."

Kara couldn't help the questions that kept popping into her mind. It was unreal, yet somehow it made sense, too. "How did you do that, send me back in time?"

T'ni Lael gestured to the time-arch. "The technology our visitors gave us."

With a sigh of resignation, Kara said, "So now, on this one day out of so many decades, you want me to try to change your world."

"It is your world as well," the Cwen replied with a determined note in her voice.

"Whatever." Kara twisted one of her curls around her finger. "So is this something where I could get hurt?"

The woman paused. "I do not think so."

"Oh, that's reassuring." Kara released the curl. "And when am I supposed to do this?"

"Tomorrow," T'ni Lael replied quietly. "On the day of *L'sen.*"

Kara's eyes locked with the woman's for one long moment. Then she pushed back her chair and stood, bracing her hands on the table.

"I'll think about it," she said, then turned and walked away.

* * * * *

After donning the snow garb that Adan had given her, Kara slipped outside into the crisp, cold air. The snowsuit was very comfortable, although she had yet to get used to the zipper that went all the way from the front to the back.

Guardcraft zipped by on maneuvers and Clan members went about their tasks from one white-walled building to another. The air chilled her face, yet it wasn't unbearably cold, and there was something about this planet that she loved. Adan came to mind and she smiled. Perhaps it was simply love for him that made this world so inviting.

She stuffed her hands into her pockets as she wandered down a road that had recently been plowed by snowcraft. Snowdrifts rose only a foot on either side of her because the roads never went as deep as the soil. Instead the Clans used some kind of spray to keep the packed snow from becoming slippery.

Kara enjoyed watching the people go about their daily tasks, and many of them waved at her as she walked by. She had become friends with several men and women since she began her stay in the village.

She did her best not to think about the Cwen and what she wanted Kara to do. Instead she thought of Adan and the countless times they had made love, the times they had gone snowmobiling—or snow-tracking as Adan called it. He had shown her around his beautiful ice-world and she found she loved it. He had taken her to the mines where they harvested gems and materials used to make structures and other items, to save snowtrees. Apparently they only used the wood from trees that toppled from the weight of snow or that were downed during larger storms.

He had also taken her to the greenhouses where they tended vegetable gardens with plants they had brought with them from Earth all those years ago. They even had one greenhouse where they grew rows and rows of corn, used to make the only bread the settlement had.

There were shops, too, such as metalworkers, bakeries, clothiers, and butchers. The latter raised a special breed of sheep brought from Earth that was the only animal hardy enough to survive the ice-planet's brutal cold—other than the world's indigenous and utterly strange animal life.

The biggest difference from what she had grown up with was that no money was exchanged. The Clan exchanged services instead, all members working in harmony for the betterment of the whole. That wasn't to say everyone got along perfectly, but what they did made sense in this harsh world.

But Kara's favorite place was the school, and she smiled at the thought. She loved working with the children, teaching them how to make crafts and helping them with their lessons. She could easily imagine herself going back to college and getting her teaching certificate so that she could teach elementary school back home. And she desperately missed the kids from the orphanage. How could she abandon them?

At that thought Kara stopped walking and frowned. How could she leave Adan and return to her old life without feeling like she'd lost a part of herself?

She walked faster, only hesitating a moment when she came to the Tower of Light. She had passed it countless times with Adan and thought it merely a monument.

Not something that could change the lives of every person on the planet.

She brought her hand to her chest. Through the thickly lined coat she could still feel the heat of the pendant between her breasts. How could one small piece of crystal be so powerful? Or was everyone here just fooled out of their gourds?

As she strolled down the snowy path she caught side of a familiar form—tall, large and powerful. As always, when outside, Adan was wearing a black snowsuit that did nothing to hide his striking physique.

Kara shivered, and it wasn't from the chill air. It amazed her how just the sight of him caused a fluttering sensation in her belly and a zing from her pussy to her nipples.

Adan was watching the crew of one of the spacecrafts, apparently supervising some kind of operation.

A sense of mischief overcame her and she bent down and scooped up some snow in her gloved hands, quickly packing it into a ball. Slowly she crept up on Adan, careful not to make a sound.

When she was close enough to see his profile, she wound her arm as if she was back on the girl's softball team, and let loose with the snowball.

It smacked square onto Adan's cheek. He whipped around and spotted her, but Kara already had another snowball ready and fired at him again, landing another blow to his stunned face.

She giggled and ran the best she could in her snow boots on the frozen road. She heard the thunder of Adan's boots behind her and she sped up—but not fast enough.

The next thing she knew, Adan had tackled her. His hands gripped her waist and she was flung flat on her back onto a clear patch of snow. He straddled her, pinning her down.

"Um, truce?" she said, trying to hold back a laugh at the sight of snow still stuck to his eyebrows and in one ear.

"Punishment is in order, woman," he said with a growl.

"Mmmm…" She glanced down to where his cock was covered by thick layers of clothing. Her gaze returned to his and she saw both amusement and desire in his dark eyes. "What kind of punishment did you have in mind?"

"You will see." Adan stood and grasped her hand, pulling her up so fast she stumbled into him. He gave her a quick searing kiss that sent warmth flooding through her, chasing away some of the chill.

He kept a tight hold on her hand as he practically dragged her through the snow to one of the greenhouses. Kara's body burned even hotter beneath her snowsuit and the pendant added to the heat flowing through her.

"What if someone is in here?" Kara said as Adan pulled her through the greenhouse door and closed it behind them.

"Then they will witness your punishment."

A thrill skipped through her belly at the thought of being watched. Not that she wanted witnesses, but the mere idea made what they were going to do all the more dangerous and exciting—whatever it was that Adan planned.

He dragged her down a pathway, between rows of vegetables until they reached a cluster of citrus trees in full bloom. He brought her behind the trees to where a long table stood.

"Bend over, put your hands on the table, and spread your legs, woman," he commanded, and Kara shivered at the authority in his voice. In normal life, she wouldn't be bossed around, but with Adan—sexually—it was such a turn-on.

She obeyed, placing her hands flat on the cool table and widening her stance.

She felt Adan's hand at the back of her snowpants, and then he zipped them down, all the way to the front, so that she was totally exposed to him.

So *that's* why they made the pants zip like that.

Kara's pussy grew wetter as he pushed aside the clothing so that her ass was bared, and he began to rub his palms over the firm flesh.

"What are you going to do, Adan?"

"Punish you." And then he spanked her with the flat of his hand.

Kara cried out in surprise. At first, the swat stung, but then she realized that it felt good, too.

"Bad girl," he murmured as he spanked first one cheek, then the other. "Bad girl."

Kara moaned, her pussy aching and begging for his cock. "Please fuck me, Adan. I promise I'll be good."

He gave a low rumble and she felt the head of his cock at the entrance to her pussy.

"That's it." Kara pushed back, trying to slide herself onto him, and he swatted her ass again.

"Ow!" she cried at the same moment he plunged his cock into her pussy. Her cry instantly became a moan of pleasure as he moved in and out of her. "You feel so good." She rocked back as he drove into her. "You're so damn big. You fill me up."

"Am I just a cock to you, woman?" he said as their flesh smacked together.

"Noooo…oh, God, that feels good."

"Then tell me again that you want *me*."

He came to a stop and leaned closer to her ear. "Come on, love, say it."

That wasn't hard at all. "I want *you*, Adan. Only you."

"That's my good girl."

The smell of her juices mingled with the scent of orange blossoms from the trees surrounding them. She heard a light scraping noise and the sound of the greenhouse door opening and closing again.

The thought of being caught send a thrill of fear and excitement through Kara. Every time they made love someplace public, it excited her. She wondered if perhaps she was a closet exhibitionist.

Her thighs trembled as they always did when she came close to climax. Adan pumped in and out of her harder and harder until stars sparked behind her eyes and she cried out with the force of her orgasm. As always, the pendant magnified her orgasm, extending it, making it almost unbearable.

Adan drove in and out several times more, extending the length of her climax until he came with a loud grunt. God, how she loved the feel of his cock throbbing inside her and the warmth that filled her after their lovemaking.

His hands moved from her hips to her waist and he bent close to her ear. "I promise you that you're mine, Kara Marks," he growled out. "Forever mine."

Chapter Fourteen

The moment she woke the following morning, Kara knew something was different. Adan's arm was wrapped around her belly, his morning erection pressed tight to her naked ass, her head tucked under his chin. It was like every other morning...but *something* was different. She could feel it simmering beneath the surface of her skin, humming through her body, and burning through the crystal that she gripped in her palm.

Adan stirred and Kara tried to wriggle out of his grasp. She needed to get up—she didn't know why, but something urged her on. When she began to slip from Adan's hold, he tightened his arm around her and nuzzled her hair. His naked body felt so good pressed to hers, and his masculine scent mixed with the smell of their sex from last night stirred an automatic desire within her.

But sex would have to wait.

"Morning, love," Adan murmured, his voice gravelly with sleep. "Since when do you wake before I do?"

Kara released her hold on her pendant and tried to pry Adan's arm from her waist. "Let me up."

He snuggled closer and hooked his leg over her hip. For one moment she was tempted to give in and have wild, passionate sex like they did every morning. But not today. Not now at least.

"I'm serious, Adan. I need to get up."

He emitted a low groan, but relaxed his hold and she squirmed out of bed.

Cool air brushed her bare flesh as she padded across the floor to the shielded window. She lightly touched it with one finger. Silently the shield shimmered and then vanished, revealing a sun swept valley.

It was beautiful. Prisms of light glinted off the Mirror Mountains and the reflection of the village, the snow-laden trees, and the frozen lake was even more vivid. The village's white walls sparkled more than ever.

Water actually dripped from the trees as some of the snow melted, and the lake glimmered as if the surface had melted, too, and she could see a patch of dark ice several feet from the shore. The underground hot springs kept the lake from completely freezing, but she had never seen the surface look like this.

And the Tower of Light—it was nothing short of amazing. It glittered, casting every color of the rainbow across the snow.

Children played around the monolith, making snow angels and having snowball fights. Their hoods were back, exposing their beautiful faces, rather than being hidden from the harsh elements like they normally were. Despite a feeling of dread in her belly, Kara had to smile at the sight of the happy children.

Not only was the outdoors a virtual wonder, but Kara's crystal pendant felt like flame against her bare chest. It didn't hurt her, but it was hot all the same.

A shiver laced Kara's spine as she sensed Adan coming up behind her. His warm breath caressed her neck and the warmth of his body heated hers, even though he wasn't touching her. He moved beside her and braced one hand on the window pane, and wrapped his other arm around her naked waist.

"In the decade I have been on Blackstar, I have never seen anything so beautiful." He tightened his hold around her waist. "Except you."

A smile touched Kara's lips, but it slipped away as the knot in her belly tightened. This was the day she was supposed to use the crystal to change the fortunes of all the planet's residents.

"I am concerned for you, love." Adan sighed as he changed the subject. "T'ni Lael assured me no harm would come to you. But she is able to wield the crystal as well." He brought her closer so that her head rested against his chest. "Turn it over to her. She has the knowledge and the power to use it. Then I will not worry that you could be in danger."

Kara gave a deep sigh. The mere thought of giving up her pendant sat like a heavy weight upon her soul.

She frowned and looked up at Adan. "What about the Ice-Witch and her people?" He cocked an eyebrow and she continued, "What if they don't want this change? It's their planet, too."

He looked thoughtful for a moment. "It would allow everyone to grow plentiful crops, we could bring other species of animals and varieties of plants through the time-arch. It would be of benefit to all."

"Are you sure?"

Adan frowned. "Why would it not?"

Kara nodded and returned her gaze to the sparkling landscape and the children playing in the snow. Deep within her soul, she knew everything was about to change. Whether for the better, she didn't know.

When the sun neared its peak for the day—its highest point until another two decades had passed—Kara and multiple Clan members moved outside to the Tower of Light. Dane and Dominik, and a host of other knights wore their laser weapons on one hip and rested their hands on the hilts of their swords strapped on the opposite side. Their gazes traveled the landscape, always on the lookout for whatever might pass the sentries and come their way.

Adan had never left her side and walked close to her, nearly suffocating her with his overpowering presence. The normally chill air felt almost warm, and the snow was slushy beneath her snow boots. The Cwen wore her emerald green robes that scrubbed the snow and dampened the hem. Somehow today Kara felt less antagonistic toward T'ni Lael. Perhaps she was finally accepting that the woman had done what she thought was best. Maybe she had been right to send Kara to Earth.

They reached the lake and the monolith, and Kara's pulse rate picked up. The only sounds were the snowbirds chirping from the hardy snowtrees, the crunch of boots on snow, and the crack of ice near the dark spot on the lake.

When they came to a stop before the monolith, T'ni Lael, ever so graceful and beautiful, broke from the small crowd. She approached the pillar, then turned to face them.

"The time has come." Her voice rang through the air, and Kara imagined it so loud it would cause an avalanche on the Mirror Mountains. "Our people will know life as it once was, countless centuries ago.

"Come, child." The Cwen motioned to Kara, who gritted her teeth at being referred to as a child. She forced herself to step forward, away from Adan's reassuring presence, conscious of every eye that was on her. She heard Adan's boot step, but T'ni Lael held up her hand. "Only Kara."

Adan caught Kara's wrist and pulled her back to him. Tension radiated from him and straight through her. "Give her the pendant," he said under his breath. "I will not allow anything to happen to you."

Kara simply nodded and Adan visibly relaxed, his features softening. "Thank you, love."

She hadn't exactly said she would give the Cwen the crystal, she had merely nodded. She wasn't sure she *could* give it to anyone. It was a part of her and the mere thought of separation left her cold.

Color from the pillar shaded T'ni Lael's features in a soft purple glow. Orange, red, yellow, and blue scattered across the snow, reminding Kara of light pouring through a stained glass window.

When Kara reached the pillar, the Cwen held out her hand. Even though her smile appeared serene, Kara noticed the lines of tension around the woman's mouth. "It is almost time," she said. "Give me the crystal."

Kara brought her hand to her chest and gripped the pendant in her palm. It burned the hottest she had ever felt it, and she almost snatched her hand away. But she couldn't if she tried. At that moment, she knew she could not give the crystal to anyone else.

Before she had a chance to say anything at all, a sudden snow flurry blinded Kara. It filled her eyes, her mouth, her nose. Shouts and cries came from the crowd, but she could see nothing. She coughed as she held her hand over her eyes and stumbled back against the pillar. She couldn't breathe without sucking snow up her nose, and the intense smell of peppermint made her sneeze.

The next thing she knew, she no longer felt snow whirling around her body, but something sharp against her neck instead. Knowing what she would find, she lowered her arm and blinked snow from her eyes to see the flurry had vanished—and there was a knife poised at her throat. The curved blade glinted in the sunlight and Kara almost screamed. She recognized Chai wielding the weapon, and the woman wore a fierce expression. A ring of ice-ghosts surrounded Kara, T'ni Lael, and the Tower of Light.

Kara's heart beat so loud it thrummed in her ears. But she could still hear the clear voice of the Ice-Witch ringing through the air as she addressed a furious Adan.

Echna removed her curved sword from its sheath, the sound of metal scraping against leather ringing out through the silent valley. Her voice came through her voicebox, low and controlled. "Order the wench to give me the crystal and I shall allow her to live."

"No!" Kara shouted and then winced as Chai pushed the point of the blade tighter against her throat. "She can't kill me. You know that."

Knowing that was true, that the ice-ghosts couldn't hurt Kara, Adan unsheathed his sword and the runes sparked with fire. No doubt this was what the Ice-Witch had been doing in her tower all these days. She had found a way to infiltrate the valley's powershielding.

In a lightning-fast movement, he swung his sword at the Ice-Witch. She met him in an easy parry with her curved blade, her moves as quick as his own.

All around them Adan's black-suited knights and Echna's white-clad ice-ghosts erupted into battle. Sounds of metal clashing against metal, grunts, and cries rang through the crisp air. The smell of battle and blood met his nose and a metallic taste filled his mouth as he fought Echna. The rush of adrenaline heightened his senses, fueled his body and sang through his sword. Beside him Dominik and Dane battled opponents almost as fierce as Echna.

Adan never let his guard down, but he was intensely aware of Kara and the ice-ghost with the blade at her throat.

Echna fought with a strength equal to his own. Her pale eyes glowed and a smile graced her lips while they parried, as if she truly enjoyed their sparring.

Every thrust she deflected, and she nearly gutted him with a lunge so fast he barely dodged it, yet it still sliced through the fabric of his snowsuit.

The sight of Kara pressed against the monument infuriated Adan. He picked up his pace, fought even harder against Echna. But she continued to match him, if not outmaneuver him. Now he had to focus entirely on the Ice-Witch to keep from being skewered.

Adan slipped on a patch of icy snow. At the same time Echna swung her booted foot out and caught Adan at the ankles. He lost his footing and his legs slid out from beneath him.

He found himself flat on his back, Echna's sword settled across his throat. "Whatever it takes, Adan Valnez, I will not allow you to harm my people."

Helplessly, Kara watched the battle as Chai kept her pinned against the pillar. The Cwen stood beside Kara, another ice-ghost guarding the woman.

Their guards divided their attention between watching Kara and T'ni Lael, keeping an eye on the battle, and being prepared for potential attackers.

"The time nears," the Cwen whispered. "To your left. There is a crevice the size of your pendant. Place the crystal there when the pillar begins to glow."

"Move and I'll cut your throat, crystal or no," Chai said, her voice as cold as the snowbound planet.

The ice-ghost pressed the point of her blade in enough to pierce Kara's flesh. She gasped and felt a drop of blood trickle down her neck.

Just a few feet behind Chai, Kara could see Adan battling Echna. Adan was an incredible swordsman, but the Ice-Witch matched him blow for blow.

Thoughts reeled through Kara's mind. How could she escape to help him?

Were the Clans and the people of Sanor right in what they wanted to do? Shouldn't the Ice-Witch and her ice-ghosts have a say in the matter, too?

Chai turned her attention to the battle, and the sword point moved slightly away from Kara's neck. Only slightly, but enough that Kara could breathe without fear of the blade digging deeper into her throat.

Her heart pounded so hard her chest ached, and she wished there was something she could do to help Adan. Anything.

To her horror, Adan went down.

It happened so fast Kara couldn't believe it. First he was on his feet battling the Ice-Witch, and the next moment he was flat on his back with Echna's sword across his throat.

Fighting around them ceased. The remaining ice-ghosts and knights held each other at sword-point, but nobody moved. Crimson stained the once beautiful snow, and bodies littered the ground.

At the same time the sunlight became brighter and the Tower of Light began to glow. Softly at first, but then slowly stronger and stronger.

"Now," T'ni Lael said in a fierce whisper. "Do it now."

All it took was those few moments for Kara's fear and fury to combine and become so intense that the pendant burned hot and fierce upon her chest. Intense heat and a flare of light burst from the crystal, slamming into Chai and throwing the ice-ghost across the battlefield, burying her in a snowbank. The warrior guarding the Cwen was flung back, too, and her sword flipped through the air, nearly driving into the ice-ghost as it fell within a fraction of her head.

Power seared Kara's veins and magnified the light and heat. She held her arms wide and her body shook as the spray of light and heat widened. It blasted into ice-ghosts and knights alike, knocking them all to the ground like bowling pins, and melting snow in a wide arc. The faces of every ice-ghost turned a brilliant shade of red as the heat overtook them.

The power slammed into Echna, throwing her back to land on her ass as her sword spun into a snowbank.

In a flash the Ice-Witch was back on her feet—her skin no longer beautiful and pale, but bright red.

Adan had made it up first, and this time his sword point was placed over Echna's heart. The symbols upon the blade glowed brighter than ever.

"Adan, don't." Kara's cry rang through the air as the light and heat faded from the pendant.

He never took his eyes off Echna. "One good reason."

"Kill her," Dane growled.

"No!" The pillar behind Kara glowed brighter, casting multicolored lights over everyone as they scrambled to their feet. Symbols appeared upon it, matching the ones on the time-arch and on Adan's sword.

"Now!" T'ni Lael's features grew more intense, no longer serene, but almost fierce. "You must complete the process now!"

"Please don't." The Ice-Witch held her head high, her gaze leveled at Kara. "My people will die if you change this world as you wish to."

"She lies." The Cwen's voice rose. She clenched her fists and glared at Kara. "Do it *now*, daughter!"

Adan's expression grew perplexed, as if realizing things were not as they seemed to be.

The colors displayed across the snow began to whirl, slowly at first, then faster and faster.

Kara's head ached and her heart pounded even harder. She grasped the crystal in one hand while she used the other to grab the chain and slip it over her head. It was painful, gut-wrenching to take the crystal from around her neck. This time the pendant was so hot she felt her skin sizzle, smelled burning flesh.

"Kill me, I care not." The Ice-Witch's voice held desperation. "But do not destroy my people."

T'ni Lael reached for Kara, trying to get to the pendant. "Do not listen to her."

Adan lowered his sword, his gaze fixed upon Kara. "You were right, love. This is their world, too."

Colors flashed faster, like they were in the middle of a kaleidoscope, and Kara's head swam. She stumbled away from the Cwen, and then ran.

She couldn't give the crystal to anyone else, but she could make sure no one would ever have it.

Kara bolted toward the lake. At the same time she wound up to pitch like she had in softball game after softball game.

She released the pendant. Pain ground through her body at the sudden loss of contact.

The crystal shot toward the lake.

In the background, T'ni Lael screamed.

The pendant landed on the smooth surface and skidded toward the hole in the ice.

Kara's heart stopped.

The crystal slid and slid, and then came to a halt at the very edge of the hole, half on, half off.

The Cwen screamed again and ran past Kara toward the lake.

"No!" Kara tried to grab T'ni Lael's robe as she ran by, but missed, the cloth just brushing her hand.

She chased after the woman—her mother—trying to stop her from running onto the ice.

The pillar's brilliant flashing lights scattered across the mostly frozen lake, becoming brighter and brighter yet. The colors illuminated the Cwen's form as she stepped onto the frozen lake's surface, slipped, and fell to her knees.

Kara ran after her, and she heard Adan's call from behind. She ignored him, trying to get to T'ni Lael before she crawled out to the weakest point on the lake.

The Cwen scrambled across the ice, nearing the hole.

Kara found herself at the edge of the lake. She dropped to her hands and knees and started scooting toward her mother.

T'ni Lael came within a foot of the pendant. She reached out and grabbed it tight in her fist.

Ice cracked as loud as thunder.

Kara screamed and pushed herself farther across the lake.

The ice gave out from beneath the Cwen.

"No!" Kara cried out as T'ni Lael plunged into the lake.

Kara tried to get close enough to grab onto the Cwen's arm, but suddenly strong arms were around her waist, pulling her back.

"No, damn it." Kara struggled against the man's hold, knowing at once that it was Adan. "I've got to get to her."

Even as she fought Adan, two ice-ghosts slipped past them, lightly treading on the frozen lake to within feet of the shattered ice. One produced a fine silver rope and lowered it into the gaping hole.

Kara held her breath, praying that her mother would grab onto the rope and that they would pull her to safety.

She waited. And waited.

All around them was complete silence. Not even the snowbirds chirped.

The colors from the Tower of Light slowly faded until there was nothing but white ice and snow around them.

Except for the one patch of black ice that her mother had fallen through.

Tears burned the corners of Kara's eyes and before she knew it, the tears rolled down her cheeks. They instantly chilled and froze upon her skin, but she barely noticed.

When they had waited for what seemed an eternity, or no time at all, the ice-ghosts looked at Kara, compassion in their pale eyes.

"She is gone," Chai said through the box at her throat.

Kara turned into Adan's embrace, let him pick her up and carry her away. She cried for a life senselessly lost. She cried for a mother she never knew. And she cried because she'd never given her mother a chance. And never forgave her while she was still alive.

Chapter Fifteen

Keiden pressed a bright synth-paper flower into Kara's palm.

"I made this for you." His adorable dimple showed when he smiled. "'Cause you're the bestest."

Kara squeezed him to her in a giant bear hug, barely avoiding crushing the paper flower between them. He smelled so good, like gingerbread and little boy. When she released Keiden, he grinned and trotted back to his desk.

For a long moment Kara watched him and the other children, her elbows on her knees and her chin propped in her hands, and listened to their chatter. She sat cross-legged on the floor in her dark blue harem pants and tunic, preparing another project for the kids to work on in the afternoon. Here she actually felt like she could make a difference in these kids' lives, that what she did mattered more than just getting a new loan for some couple refinancing their home. The only thing she had done at home that seemed to matter was stopping by the orphanage and playing with the kids.

Soon she had to make her decision.

Could she leave the children?

Could she leave Adan?

She moved her hands from her chin, opened her right hand, and studied her palm. An imprint of the pendant had been permanently seared into her flesh. Thanks to the

Clans' technology the wound had already healed, but a vivid pink scar remained.

The scar would always remind her of her mistakes. And of the things she managed to get right.

The week following the accident had passed in a blur for Kara. Two days after T'ni Lael's death, the Clans had a simple traditional ceremony. The people of Sanor refused to join them and performed their own ritual deep in the bowels of the planet where they had lived for over two decades.

After the death rites, the Clans had held a communal feast to celebrate the Cwen's life and her contribution to the people of Sanor and the three Clans. During the feast Kara hadn't been able to bring herself to celebrate anything. She blamed herself for her mother's death. She believed she had been right in not allowing the world-change to take place, but by throwing the pendant into the lake, she had inadvertently caused T'ni Lael's death.

Now that a week had passed — with her work with the Clans' children and Adan's love to ease her pain — Kara had begun to forgive herself. There was nothing she could do about it now, but she still felt some guilt and grief at not trying to get to know her mother better, at not forgiving her for doing what she had thought was the right thing. Maybe she *had* saved Kara's life all those years ago when she sent her to live on Earth.

No, nothing had been like it seemed to be. Even the ice-ghosts hadn't truly been evil. They had only wanted to save their own lives.

Kara snatched a pair of scissors from the floor beside her, and rounded a corner off a piece of red synth-paper.

One good thing she had accomplished was to help the Clans form a treaty with the Ice-Witch and her ice-ghosts. Adan had told Kara he didn't think any love would be lost between their people, but he rested easier knowing a bond of peace now existed between them. But, he wasn't about to lower his guard, wasn't about to allow the Clans to be unprepared—just in case.

Kara rounded another corner off the paper, made a V-cut, then snipped off two sides. When she was done she held a bright red heart in her hands. Next thing she knew she would be writing "Kara loves Adan" on it.

And she did. More than anything.

Her gaze flicked from the heart back to the students busy writing their vocabulary words on synth-paper. The Clans had the technology for the students to use only electronic devices for their schoolwork, but they wanted to preserve the past in small ways, so their children could read and write with writing utensils and synth-paper.

Kara's gaze fixed on Keiden and a tight feeling wound itself in her heart. A feeling of pride, joy, and love, as if he was her son. What would it be like to have a child of her own, to feel that precious life growing in her womb and to cherish every moment of her child's life?

She could only imagine having a child with Adan. Could only imagine being in his arms forevermore.

Kara rubbed one hand over her modest harem pants, the dark silk-like material soothing against the scar on her palm. What about her friends Jan and Sheri? Would she be allowed to say goodbye to them, to let them know what happened to her? Surely Adan could let her use the time-arch. Maybe Jan and Sheri would visit the orphanage for her. They had expressed interest, hadn't they? What about her job, her life back on Earth? Her job had never been as fulfilling as her work with the children of Blackstar, and her life had been beyond dull. And her friends — she loved them, but she loved Adan even more.

Truly, in her heart, she knew there had been no real doubt. She had just been scared to take that step. It seemed so final, so complete, severing her ties with all that she had ever known. But she had absolutely no doubt any more...her place was here on Blackstar, at Adan's side. On Earth, her two friends had been all the family she'd known. Here, she felt like she had an entire extended family including the children, their parents, the knights, and everyone she'd met. And Adan. Of course, Adan.

The sound of boot steps jerked her attention from the children to the doorway, and her heart nearly exploded with joy at seeing Adan. Impulsively, she jumped up and ran to meet him. Almost without thought, she climbed him, wrapping her arms and legs around his waist.

"I love you, Adan Valnez." She pressed her forehead to his. "I could never ever leave you."

The look that came over his masculine features was one of fierce joy, amazement, and love.

"I thought I would have to chain you to my side," he said in a husky growl. "You are *mine*, Kara Marks."

Their lips met in a hungry, anxious kiss. His tongue made love to hers as if he couldn't get enough of her. She knew she would never get enough of him.

She was so lost in the warmth of his arms around her, the feel of his body pressed tight to hers, the intensity of his kiss, and his intoxicating scent, that she lost touch with time and reality.

Gradually she became aware of small voices in the background, children laughing and chattering.

"Ewww, yuck," said one little boy.

"That's dee-scusting," said another.

A girl said, "I think Clan Leader Valnez is going to marry Ms. Marks."

Mrs. Night's "ah-hem" rang through the room as Kara and Adan pulled apart. Kara's cheeks burned and she was tempted to bury her face against Adan's shirt.

He smiled and looked to the classroom. "Aye. I am going to marry Ms. Marks."

"That means she's going to stay here on Blackstar, doesn't it?" asked a hopeful-sounding Keiden.

Kara smiled at him. "Yes."

The class erupted into cheers. As Adan carried Kara through the doorway, she heard Keiden say, "I guess it's okay if they kiss, if it will make Ms. Marks stay."

She laughed and Adan could not help but grin like a besotted fool. He wanted to shout to the skies, to every star, to every person and every living thing on this world.

He could not reach their chambers fast enough. Kara nibbled at his neck and made small sounds of pleasure as he carried her through the many hallways. Too many hallways. He nearly mowed down two junior knights, Dominik, and a pleasure-partner, in his rush to get his woman to his room.

When they reached the chamber door Kara moved her lips to the corner of his mouth. When he placed his hand to the ID screen, the door slid up. He kissed her and they stumbled inside.

Their lips locked in a wild and passionate dance as the door lowered behind them. He dropped to his knees and pressed her back against the floor. Fire burned in his loins, and his cock was hard enough to drill though gemstones.

Her mouth tore away from his and she kissed a trail from his lips to the line of his jaw. "Fuck me, Adan."

"No." He captured her face between his palms, halting her kisses and forcing her to look at him. "Make love to you."

"Yes." Her pussy was so wet and her nipples so hard, she couldn't wait to get him inside of her.

Adan ground his mouth against hers, bruising her lips. His stubble chafed her skin and his hands slid into her curls. Kara kissed back with all the intensity of her desire, of her love.

They both made sounds of pleasure, groans and soft moans. Adan rolled onto his back, and brought her on top, straddling him, her pussy pressed against his cock. Kara tore her mouth from his and stared down at his strong features. She brought her thumb to his mouth and gasped as he caught it between his teeth in a soft bite.

"I love everything about you." She spread her fingers over his cheek, feeling the sandpaper-rough stubble against the pads of her fingers. "The way you treat me like a precious treasure, the way your eyes soften when you see children. I love the respect your people have for you, and the way you return that respect. I love how firm you are in your leadership, yet how gentle and kind you can be, too. On the outside you're a big ol' bear, but inside you're a nothing but a softie."

Adan grunted, but she could see the pleasure in his eyes.

He held onto her and rolled her so that she was on her back and he was between her thighs again.

She met his intense expression, those dark eyes filled with such emotion it almost brought her to tears.

"You are everything to me." Adan's tone was gruff, as if he was choked with emotion. "I love the way you smile, your laughter. I love your courage, your strength." He gave a little grin. "Your temper, too."

Kara gave him a playful swat.

His expression grew serious again. "I love how you care for those around you, how you treat the Clans' children as if they were your own. I love your strength of character and how you made the right choice—a choice I was too blind to see until it was almost too late—to save a race of people. I love everything about you, Kara Marks."

She had never experienced such sheer joy in her life as she did at that moment.

Their eyes remained locked as Adan rose up, took Kara's hand, and eased her to her feet as he stood. He brought her palm to his lips and she gasped when he flicked his tongue over the scar. Still holding her, he moved his free hand to the curl at her forehead. He gave it a little tug, let it spring back into place, and gave her a crooked smile.

The memory of the first time they had met washed over her. How he had studied her, how he had touched her like he was now. They had come full circle.

Adan pulled away and led her to the bed. They stood beside it, just holding hands for a moment.

He released her to brush his knuckles across her cheek, over her jaw and down the curve of her throat. Kara shivered as his fingers met the cloth of her tunic and he traced her skin along the neckline, and then trailed one finger lazily down between her breasts... A slow, sensual exploration that took her breath away.

She couldn't wait for him, but she didn't want him to hurry. She loved this side of him, the gentleness and sensuality he showed when they were alone. He was a fierce warrior, her honorable knight, and her passionate, caring lover.

Adan brought his hands to the hem of her tunic and carefully brought it up as she helped him remove it. She stood before him, her nipples tightening beneath his fiery gaze.

"You are such a beauty, inside, as well as out." His palm rested on one of her breasts, the heat of his hand driving wild sensations through her core.

Kara could barely breathe. His words, the way he touched her, it was incredible. He continued his exploration of her body, as if touching her, seeing her for the first time. He caressed his rough hands over her soft skin, trailed his mouth and tongue along her curves, and sucked on her nipples until she could barely stand to take such sweet torture any longer.

He hooked his fingers in the waistband of her harem pants and peeled them off inch by aching inch. As he did, he nuzzled her mound and breathed deeply of her scent as she moaned.

Gripping her hips in his large palms, Adan began exploring her belly, hips, and thighs with his mouth. Her legs trembled and her heart pounded out a steady rhythm.

When his tongue found her folds, she cried out and nearly dropped to her knees. He licked her in long hungry strokes, a low growl emanating from him. Pleasure built up in her, winding tighter and tighter, until it exploded and her cry ripped through the room.

While Kara still shook from her orgasm, Adan rose up until he again towered over her.

His cock jerked in his breeches as he studied her passion-glazed eyes and her flushed cheeks.

"I wish for you to taste what I taste, the sweetness of your essence," he said as he lowered his lips, moist with her juices, to her mouth.

She gave soft moan and opened for him, as his lips met hers. He gripped her shoulders tight within his hands, as he devoured her, tasted her juices, tasted all of her.

When they broke away, Kara tugged at the hem of his tunic. "I think *I'll* take over from here."

The corner of his mouth twitched at the seriousness of her expression. He helped her remove his tunic, then clenched his fists at his sides as she began her own exploration. Adan bit the inside of his cheek, forcing himself to hold back from taking Kara now. He allowed her to take her time, to kiss and nibble and lick his flesh. By the skies, her lips were so soft, her tongue so wet and warm. She lightly scraped her teeth down his abs and he sucked in his breath as she neared his waistband. He thanked the skies that her fingers were nimble as she unfastened his breeches, freeing his cock. He had barely been able to breathe, as tight as the cloth had constricted him.

Kara sighed and got to her knees. "Such a perfect specimen of manhood." She glanced up with a teasing smile and her tongue darted along her lips. "I can't wait to taste you."

He was certain he could not wait either.

But instead of sliding her mouth over his cock, she pushed his breeches down, trailing her tongue along his skin, doing what he had done to her.

He was definitely regretting his earlier erotic torture of Kara. At least his cock was.

When she finally grasped his erection in her small hand and licked the head of his cock, his groan reverberated throughout his chambers.

"Serves you right, you know," she said, giving his cock another swipe of her tongue. And then, before he could respond, she slid her mouth over his length and all thought vanished from his mind.

Her mouth — so hot, so wet, so welcoming. She moved her hand in tandem with her mouth, stroking the sensitive skin of his shaft. She fondled his balls, caressing them lightly, causing him to groan from the sheer pleasure of it.

Kara sucked him until he could take it no more. He pulled his cock from her mouth then reached down, caught her by the waist, and laid her on the bed.

The bed covering was soft to Kara's back, but the man sliding between her thighs was rock-hard muscle. He braced himself over her, his long hair falling over his shoulders to caress her nipples.

His eyes said everything. Told her how much he cared for her, loved her. And she knew her eyes reflected that love right back to him. It filled her heart and soul with such happiness it was almost painful.

"Let me in, love," he murmured as he put the head of his cock at the entrance to her core.

"You already are," she whispered.

Adan plunged into her and held still. She gasped at the sensation of him stretching her, filling her. No matter how many times they had made love, this moment was always delicious — when he entered her and made her his.

In slow steady strokes, Adan began to fuck her. No, *make love* to her.

Spirals of pleasure whirled through her, intertwining with the love she felt for Adan. She thrust up to meet him at every stroke, holding back her orgasm as long as she could, wanting to make this time last forever.

She could see the fine rein of control in his eyes, the tenseness of his jaw. Sweat rolled down his brow and their perspiration mingled as their bodies met with each thrust.

Kara's climax built and built and built. The spirals of pleasure became more intense, and colors swirled in her mind. She could no longer think, could only feel.

"Join me, love," Adan said. "Come with me."

The spirals of pleasure burst from Kara and all she saw was prisms of light. Her cry echoed through the room, joining with Adan's as his cock pulsed within her core. This was far, far more amazing than her climaxes had been with the pendant. Now it was her love for Adan that made it so very incredible. So much better than ever before.

As her orgasm slowly faded, Adan's face gradually came back into focus. He was breathing hard, his gaze locked on her with that soul-deep look that melted her very soul.

Kara smiled up at him. "You know I intend to make you keep your promise, don't you?"

He cocked an eyebrow. "What promise?"

She brushed a long strand of hair away from his brow. "That I'm yours forever and ever."

"Love, that's a promise I intend to keep for eternity."

Enjoy this excerpt from
KING OF CLUBS
© Copyright Cheyenne McCray 2004

Chapter One

Awai Steele paced the length of her condominium, her heels sinking into the deep, lush burgundy carpeting. She preferred not to wear a bra when she wasn't working, and the silky material of her blouse rasped her nipples, making them taut with hunger. Her short skirt brushed her upper thighs and the falling star at her belly button swung against her flat belly.

The condo smelled of carpet shampoo, pine cleaner, and fresh paint. It was bare of all furnishings, everything put into long-term storage.

Because tonight *they* would come for her.

Awai wrapped her fingers tighter around the handle of her leather whip and snapped the long strip of leather, the crack loud and satisfying. It was exactly a year since Annie vanished, two years for Alexi, and three years to the day that Alice had disappeared.

Without a doubt Awai knew she was next.

"Let them come," she murmured and snapped her whip again. She didn't know who had taken her nieces, but whoever they were, they would pay dearly if the girls had come to any harm.

After Annie and her cat Abracadabra had vanished, Awai spent the year preparing for today. The first thing she did was put all of Annie's belongings into storage with Alexi's and Alice's possessions. Then gradually throughout the year, Awai sold her advertising agency along with all her shares of stock, her condo, and her Mercedes SL600. Every penny Awai owned, totaling well over five million dollars, was in an account earmarked for a women's shelter that aided victims of domestic violence. If Awai didn't return within a specified amount of time, the funds would go to the shelter. Her estate and her nieces' belongings would be taken out of storage and given to the same facility.

Awai paused in her pacing and moved to the expansive window that stretched along two sides of the large common room. Her view of San Francisco was magnificent, and tonight was no exception. City lights glittered in the darkness and so did the lights along the Golden Gate Bridge. No doubt she would miss this view, wherever she was going, but she missed her nieces more. A constant ache had taken residence in her heart and soul, and she wouldn't rest until she found Annie, Alice, and Alexi.

Awai was only a few years older than her nieces, being their aunt by marriage. Long ago she had married the girls' distant uncle, John Steele—

And the bastard had nearly killed her.

A hard and cold knot expanded in Awai's gut like it did every time she thought of the son of a bitch. She had been young, innocent, and fresh out of high school when she met John. He had wooed her with his charm and expensive gifts, and had seduced her into his bed.

Awai ran the leather strap of her whip over her palm as her thoughts turned back to that horrid time in her life and her triumph in making a new life for herself.

Once she escaped the bastard, she'd promised herself that no man would ever dominate her again.

Awai raised her chin, no longer seeing the city lights, but instead the light of her past. With her intelligence and drive, Awai had quickly worked her way to the top of her profession in the advertising business. Eventually she had started her own firm, and it wasn't long before she was drawing in larger and larger accounts until her agency was one of the premier advertising firms in the state of California. She became known as a ball buster, the woman with brass ovaries. She didn't take shit from any man, and her staff was populated almost exclusively with women.

She had also started an extensive training program in the domestic violence shelter. With Awai's financial backing, the center taught women skills necessary to enter the workforce. Frequently, Awai hired women from the shelter in positions such as receptionist or filing clerk. Gradually, as they learned the ropes, many of the women were trained in more demanding tasks and worked their way up through the advertising agency.

Awai shifted and lightly flicked her whip, allowing it to curl like a sensuous caress around her bare legs and the leather straps from her heels that wrapped around her ankles and calves.

There was another side to her life that no one knew about outside of her niece Annie. Almost every evening, Awai left her daily concerns and entered the world of BDSM as a Dominatrix, as Mistress Awai.

Awai treated her submissives well, making sure they enjoyed the erotic play, and always keeping the relationships safe, sane, and consensual. She had chosen to become a Domme simply because she had made that promise to herself…that no man would be her Master.

Yet something was missing. She couldn't quite place her finger on it, but she didn't feel complete being a

Domme. Awai knew what she wanted in life and went after it with a vengeance. So why was her role as a Domme not entirely satisfying?

As if I wished to be the one tied up and at a male Dom's mercy.

She shrugged away the errant thought. *What the hell's the matter with me?*

Awai moved away from the window, a sense of melancholy rolling over her. She was known as a take-charge dynamo, and these feelings of confusion were pissing her off. Yet, as she thought more and more about being a Domme, and of her missing nieces, she felt both angry and brooding...and regretful.

Awai snapped her whip in the empty room, the crack of leather jarring her back into her role. She would take charge and let the bastards who stole her nieces know who was boss.

When will they get here? she wondered as she stared at the front door. It was well after ten—only two hours left until midnight and then the anniversary of all her nieces' disappearances would have passed.

Awai frowned at the stately mahogany door. *Could I have been wrong?*

No. She wouldn't allow doubt to make her insecure. Everything in her gut told her that they would be coming for her, too.

Since there wasn't any furniture left in the condo, Awai moved to the wall beside the door. She slid down the wall until she was sitting in the plush burgundy carpeting and set her whip beside her. Awai's short skirt hiked up to her waist and her thong pulled tight against her clit. It had been days since she'd had a fuck, and for some reason the last one hadn't been as fulfilling as she'd hoped.

A wild fantasy had gone through her mind as she'd had sex with her sub. A fantasy of riding a powerful man, his cock filling her pussy while another man slid his erection into her ass. And yet a third grabbing her by her hair and forcing her to suck his cock. She was totally at their mercy while all three men fucked her.

At the memory of the fantasy, Awai couldn't help but slide one hand down to her pussy. As she visualized the scene again, she moved aside the thong and fingered her clit. With her free hand she pushed her blouse above her pert breasts, exposing her nipples to the cool air in the condo.

She started out with small circles around her clit then thrust one finger into her pussy, then spread her juices over her folds. Against her will, she found herself back in the fantasy of the three men. This time one of the men was eating her pussy while another one kissed her, and the third sucked her nipples.

The thought of three gorgeous men focused on her pleasure, and in turn her pleasuring them, sent Awai into orbit. Her orgasm came hard and fast, and caused her to moan as ripple after ripple of her climax continued to flow through her until she came a second time.

After she slipped her hand from her thong and arranged her clothing a bit, Awai relaxed against the wall and closed her eyes. She brought her fingers to her nose and scented herself, wondering what it would be like to smell the come of three men all at once.

What's the matter with me? Why am I fantasizing about dominant men? I should think instead of the men I dominate.

But the men continued to haunt her. Awai sighed and sank deeper into her thoughts until she slipped into a deep but unsettling sleep.

A blond god of a man tied Awai's wrists together with a glittering golden rope. It was snug, yet the rope didn't hurt or cut into her flesh. In a sensuous caress, he slid his hands down her thighs and calves then bound her ankles together too, with another piece of the golden rope. When he finished, he lowered his head to the juncture of her thighs and inhaled deeply, his long blond hair caressing her skin. He gave a satisfied purr, like a tiger, and she felt a tingle in her pussy and her panties grew wet.

Awai jerked awake and found herself still positioned with her back to the wall of her condo. She blinked, feeling oddly disoriented and almost as if she'd been drugged.

Golden light shone across the living room carpet, yet through the windows in front of her she could still see San Francisco's sparkling nighttime view. Slowly she turned her head and saw that the door was open —

Sunlight was spilling into her home. Not a hall light or a streetlight. It was pure butter yellow sunshine like on a cool spring morning in places where there wasn't any fog to dim it.

Her heart pounded like mad. She tried to get to her feet, only to slide down the wall and fall onto her side, her cheek resting on the leather handle of her whip.

Her hands and ankles were bound, just like in her dream.

Awai's breathing was hard and fast as she glanced at the golden rope around her wrists and then looked to her ankles.

A shadow fell across the carpet.

Awai's gaze shot to the doorway and she saw the golden god from her dreams. The man's white-blond hair tumbled over his shoulders and a gold earring glittered in one ear. His muscled chest was bare, and the tattoo of a club was on his magnificent six-pack abs. Good lord, but those leather pants cradled his impressive family jewels, and despite the fact she was tied up and at his mercy, Awai's pussy tingled.

Instead of the diatribe she had planned when "they" finally showed up to kidnap her, Awai found herself absolutely speechless.

The golden god flexed his muscles as he moved closer then knelt before her on one knee. His intense blue eyes focused on her and he smelled of sun-warmed flesh and mountain air. Gently he brushed the back of his hand over her cheek, and in a voice that sent shivers down her spine, the god said, "I have come for you."

About the Cheyenne McCray:

Cheyenne McCray is a thirty-something wild thing at heart, with a passion for sensual romance and a happily-ever-after...but always with a twist. A University of Arizona alumnus, Chey has been writing ever since she can remember, back to her kindergarten days when she penned her first poem. She always knew that one day she would write novels, and with her love of fantasy and romance, combined with her passionate nature, erotic romance is a perfect genre for her. In addition to her adult work, Chey is also published in young adult literary fiction under another name. Chey enjoys spending time with her husband and three sons, traveling, working out at the health club, playing racquetball, and of course writing, writing, writing.

Cheyenne welcomes mail from readers. You can write to her c/o Ellora's Cave Publishing at 1337 Commerce Drive, Suite 13, Stow OH 44224.

Why an electronic book?

We live in the Information Age—an exciting time in the history of human civilization in which technology rules supreme and continues to progress in leaps and bounds every minute of every hour of every day. For a multitude of reasons, more and more avid literary fans are opting to purchase e-books instead of paperbacks. The question to those not yet initiated to the world of electronic reading is simply: *why?*

1. *Price.* An electronic title at Ellora's Cave Publishing runs anywhere from 40-75% less than the cover price of the <u>exact same title</u> in paperback format. Why? Cold mathematics. It is less expensive to publish an e-book than it is to publish a paperback, so the savings are passed along to the consumer.

2. *Space.* Running out of room to house your paperback books? That is one worry you will never have with electronic novels. For a low one-time cost, you can purchase a handheld computer designed specifically for e-reading purposes. Many e-readers are larger than the average handheld, giving you plenty of screen room. Better yet, hundreds of titles can be stored within your new library—a single microchip. (Please note that Ellora's Cave does not endorse any specific brands. You can check our website at www.ellorascave.com for customer recommendations we make available to new consumers.)

3. *Mobility.* Because your new library now consists of only a microchip, your entire cache of books can be taken with you wherever you go.

4. *Personal preferences are accounted for.* Are the words you are currently reading too small? Too large? Too...**ANNOYING**? Paperback books cannot be modified according to personal preferences, but e-books can.

5. *Innovation.* The way you read a book is not the only advancement the Information Age has gifted the literary community with. There is also the factor of what you can read. Ellora's Cave Publishing will be introducing a new line of interactive titles that are available in e-book format only.

6. *Instant gratification.* Is it the middle of the night and all the bookstores are closed? Are you tired of waiting days—sometimes weeks—for online and offline bookstores to ship the novels you bought? Ellora's Cave Publishing sells instantaneous downloads 24 hours a day, 7 days a week, 365 days a year. Our e-book delivery system is 100% automated, meaning your order is filled as soon as you pay for it.

Those are a few of the top reasons why electronic novels are displacing paperbacks for many an avid reader. As always, Ellora's Cave Publishing welcomes your questions and comments. We invite you to email us at service@ellorascave.com or write to us directly at: 1337 Commerce Drive, Suite 13, Stow OH 44224.

Discover for yourself why readers can't get enough of the multiple award-winning publisher Ellora's Cave. Whether you prefer e-books or paperbacks, be sure to visit EC on the web at www.ellorascave.com for an erotic reading experience that will leave you breathless.

WWW.ELLORASCAVE.COM

Printed in the United States
26318LVS00005B/136-291

9 781419 951084